FATED IN RUBY

Blood Oath #4

J.A. CARTER

Fated in Ruby

Published by J.A. Carter

Copyright © 2022 by J.A. Carter

www.authorjacarter.com

Cover Design: Keylin Rivers

ALSO BY J.A. CARTER

Blood Oath Series

Bound in Crimson

Tempted by Fire

Entangled in Scarlet

Fated in Ruby

Unraveled by Desire

BLURB

I never had a say in my future—until now.

When the truth about the blood oath is revealed, Calla has a devastating choice to make: leave the vampires she's caught feelings for or stay and fight for the life she's built with them. And each choice has severe, irreversible consequences.

With the hunters at large, carrying out attacks of their own, and a betrayal by someone close to Calla, she remains stuck in a whirlwind of fear and confusion. Not to mention the darkness still lurking in Kade or the psychotic vampire Selene lurking in the shadows.

Faced with a life-altering ultimatum, Calla must choose to give up everything she has come to know or the future she is terrified to want.

For you, the reader.

1

LEX

New York City, a long fucking time ago...

The street is quieter than normal. The quiet that comes from thick, heavy snowfall, muting the sounds of people and cars. The air is so cold my lungs sting with each fogged breath as I hurry down the slick sidewalk toward the parking garage a few blocks away from my office building. My face is frozen, and I curse the white shit covering my path... and my decision not to park closer to the office this morning. Considering my odds of getting a spot on the street in the downtown core were slim, I hadn't bothered wasting my time driving around. I'd overslept and really fucking needed a coffee.

I pick up my pace, jogging down the cement steps into the parking garage, my messenger bag bouncing against my hip.

It takes three tries for my engine to turn over, and I toss my bag onto the passenger seat, cranking the heat before backing out of my spot and heading toward the street.

The road conditions get worse as I make it out of the city toward the bridge, and I—for approximately the millionth time since I started working for my company three years ago—regret not spending the extra money to get a townhouse in the city.

Cranking the heat higher, I drum my fingers against the steering wheel to the soft rock song on the radio. Messing with the tuner, I try to find a station that will come through clearly, but most are static and cutting out from the weather.

I take my eyes off the snow-covered road for a second. And a second is all it takes.

A horn blares.

I slam the brakes.

The car doesn't stop. In fact, the packed snow under my tires makes them slide, sending my car across the lane—straight into the traffic traveling in the opposite direction.

I don't have a moment to react or even a second to close my eyes or yell.

Everything happens at once. The truck slams into me, shattering the windshield. The airbags blow, knocking the air out of my lungs, and my head snaps back against the seat so violently the world darkens to nothing.

I don't know how much time passes.

Am I dead?

I don't think I'm dead.

I can't hear or see anything.

The reason I don't think I'm dead? Everything hurts like hell. A pain so intense it might actually be keeping me alive, if that's even possible.

Cold seeps through me, and slowly—so fucking slowly—the sounds of horns blaring and people shouting break through the ringing in my ears. Everything is muffled, and I can't seem to remember how to open my eyes. Wetness drips down my face. I groan. At least, I think I do. Or maybe I'm screaming. Crying out for help from the darkness threatening to steal me away.

I'm scared. Scared I'm going to let it take me without a fight, because anything has to be better than the agony I'm in.

Glass trickles in from somewhere, hitting the dash as the sharp scent of copper mixed with burning rubber assaults my nose.

At some point, I manage to pry my eyes open.

There's a man at my side, standing in the open door.

Oh. The door isn't open—it's gone.

His eyes are too light and his lips are turned down into a frown. He looks angry and confused and sad all at once. When he opens his mouth, I can't hear the words he's saying. Shaking his head, he leans inside the car, pressing himself so close, my body explodes with white-hot pain.

"... shattered nearly... bone... your..."

My skull is pounding, but as the seconds tick by—or maybe it's minutes or hours—the pain fades into numbness, and I can't help but fear that isn't a good thing. I want the pain back. It means I'm still alive.

"...going... be dead... the next... if I... something. I... help"

His hands cup both sides of my neck, holding my head up despite it wanting to fall back against the seat.

I struggle to focus on his face. The harsh lines of his jaw, his defined brows, the dark stubble on his cheeks. The vision of him blurs, ebbing in and out.

My eyes flit to his mouth when he speaks again. I think he asks for my name. But when I open my mouth to respond, nothing comes out.

The man nods. "...figure... later." He flicks his tongue across his lips, and I blink at the sight of his elongated canines.

I've fucking lost it. I'm seeing a man with fangs standing in front of me while I die.

I always joked about going to hell, but perhaps it's really happening, and this guy is going to take me there.

He moves in a blur, sinking those impossibly sharp fangs into my neck.

I don't move, don't make a sound. The pain I would expect to feel having someone tear into my throat doesn't exist in my reality.

In fact, after a few seconds, there's a trickle of warmth that seeps into my veins. I close my eyes against it, clinging to that tiny bit of pleasure in this nightmare.

And then he grips my jaw, forcing my mouth open and pouring in something warm and thick.

My eyes pop open to find his wrist pressed against my lips.

His blood. I'm drinking his blood.

I don't have the strength to stop myself from swallowing mouthfuls of the coppery liquid.

After I swallow a few times, he pulls his wrist back, and I catch sight of the puncture marks before they disappear, as if they were never there.

Sirens echo in the distance, getting closer, and I blink at the man who both drank my blood and fed me his, in utter confusion.

"... part isn't... be... pleasant... I'm sorry... make it quick."

I don't have time to grasp his words before he reaches for me once more and ends it all in one fatal motion.

☙❧

If this is what hell feels like, I should have been more concerned about ending up here. My entire being hurts so deep it's otherwise indescribable. Darkness surrounds me and my veins are filled with liquid fire. My head is pounding with what feels like a splitting migraine and my throat is full of sandpaper.

"Alexander."

Someone is calling my name from far away. The voice is muffled and deep... and vaguely familiar. I've heard it once before.

I try to speak, but nothing comes out.

"You need to drink."

Yes. Water. I need water.

Reaching blindly, still unable to pry my eyes open against the pain paralyzing me, I grunt when my hands hit a solid wall of muscle.

"Open your eyes," the voice demands, and it's as if I needed him to tell me to, because I manage to do what he says.

My eyes are immediately overwhelmed, trying to focus on everything at once. The man sitting in front of me, the luxurious space we're in, the darkness outside the window across the room. I get stuck on the woman sitting off to the side. She can't be much older than twenty. I'm only in my mid-twenties, but still. She looks uncomfortable and out of place here. But she smells absolutely amazing.

What the fuck?

My eyes snap back to the man and widen as my brows scrunch together.

"It's okay," he assures me.

I swallow, wincing at the pain scratching at my throat. "What," I force out, "happened?"

The man frowns briefly. "Long story short, you died. Sorry."

My heart lurches at the same time my stomach drops, and I feel as if I'm going to vomit all over this guy in a second.

"There was an accident. Your car slid into oncoming traffic and you were hit head-on by a truck. I was driving behind it and saw the accident happen."

I'm actually fucking dead?

"So this is hell?"

His lips twitch for a split second. "Depending on how you look at it, I suppose it could be."

I blink at him. "Huh?"

"I'll explain everything, but you need to drink first."

My eyes drift back to the woman. "Who's she?"

"Your dinner," he answers simply. "You'll feel much better once you drink."

My eyes widen again, and I try to move away from him, though the second I do, pain flares through me, stopping any further movement. "You're crazy," I stutter.

"Many would agree," he offers. "I'm Atlas. Also, a vampire, as you will be once you drink and complete the transition."

Suddenly things start to come back. The crash. This man. His fangs.

"You... you killed me!"

He scoffs. "I saved your life, actually. You're welcome."

I drag my hands down my face, my fingers cold and shaking. "I don't want to be a vampire." My voice is empty, tone vacant.

"You'd rather be dead?" He shrugs. "Fine. Don't drink. I really don't need the hassle of siring someone anyway."

I shake my head, which doesn't help the spinning. "I don't... What are you...?" I can't finish a fucking sentence at this point.

The man—Atlas, apparently—sighs heavily. "To become a vampire, you need to die with both vampire venom and blood in your system, which you did. Then you come back to life in a sort of in-between state, which you have. You either drink human blood and become a vampire, or the pain you're feeling will get worse until you ultimately die. Again. For good."

I grit my teeth. "Why?"

"That is a very loaded question, Alexander. One with several possible answers. Are you asking why vampires exist, or why I chose to turn you into one?"

Another wave of fiery pain flares through me, and I grip the sides of my head, squeezing my eyes shut and groaning. "Why did you do this to me?"

Atlas inhales deeply. "I... am not quite sure yet." He stands and approaches the woman, offering her his hand, which she takes immediately, before walking back to me. The woman sits next to me while Atlas remains standing.

"You... you want me to drink her blood?" I force out, wincing at the dryness in my throat.

He grabs the woman's wrist, lifting it to his mouth and biting into it without hesitation. She sucks in a breath, then sighs softly, closing her eyes and falling against the back of the couch. Atlas

6

pulls back after a moment and offers me her wrist, seemingly unconcerned that her blood is dripping onto the hardwood.

"Time to choose," he says in a flat but not unkind voice. "Drink now and live forever, or don't and die."

My eyes hone in on the blood pooling around the puncture marks on her wrist. Somehow I can smell it, and the harsh copper scent is making my gums throb, filling my head with a haze of... hunger.

I'm moving before I can stop myself, cradling the woman's wrist in my hands, lifting it to my mouth. I close my eyes, pressing my lips to her skin and trailing my tongue along Atlas's bite mark. The second I taste her blood, my veins sing with relief. The pain disappears instantly, and I moan at its absence, drinking deeply. The woman's blood flows easily, filling my mouth, and with every swallow, I feel stronger. Within seconds, the throbbing in my gums intensifies to an uncomfortable level. Before I know what's happening, fangs slice through, and I pull away from the woman's wrist only to tug her closer to me and sink my new, lethally sharp teeth into her neck.

She cries out, but the sound is quickly replaced by a lust-filled moan.

I swallow mouthfuls of her hot, thick blood, growling deep in my throat as the sound of her pounding heartbeat fills my ears. The longer I drink, the more it slows. I don't stop—I can't.

I lose track of time, of everything but the taste of life exploding on my tastebuds.

And then Atlas says, "Stop now or she'll die."

I don't care.

"Alexander." His tone sharpens.

I don't care. I don't stop.

Atlas sighs.

The woman's heart slows until I can't hear it anymore. Until it stops beating.

"She's dead," Atlas says mildly.

Finally, I pull back. I blink at the sight of the woman slouched against the couch, blood dripping from her neck and her eyes rolled into the back of her head.

Fucking hell.

I just killed someone.

I'm... a monster.

"What..." I choke on the word, lifting my hand to my mouth, and gasp when my finger touches a razor-sharp canine.

Atlas shrugs, unbothered. "It happens. Don't worry about it. Most vampires kill their first feed."

"I... I didn't mean to." I wipe my mouth with the back of my hand.

"The hunger will control you if you don't learn to understand it. There is much you will need to learn, Alexander. Your life as a human is over. Consider this your rebirth."

I frown at my name. It doesn't feel like me anymore.

Alexander died in that car.

"You're looking at me strangely."

Exhaling slowly, I lift my gaze to his. It's the first time I've noticed his eyes are silver. "I don't think I want to be Alexander."

He nods. "What would you like me to call you then?"

I scratch the back of my neck. I don't think I'm ready to part with my old life as much as I'd like to believe I am. "Lex," I finally say. "I want to be called Lex."

2

CALLA

The soft, steady *beep, beep, beep* from the monitor Mom is attached to is driving me crazy. I've been pacing her hospital room for almost an hour, my Docs squeaking against the pale beige tile each time I turn and switch direction. It isn't making me feel better, but I sure as hell can't sit still. My stomach is a mess of nerves and my head is spinning. Every time I try to wrap my head around the news that I'm not the firstborn Montgomery daughter, my pulse jackhammers and a wave of nausea-filled panic floods through me. And the thought of the guys having over-heard the conversation terrifies me. They're keeping their distance, but they can't be far. Which means, if they were listening, they know.

What does this mean for me—for us?

If the oath is void, if it was never mine to fulfill... will they let me go?

Do I *want* them to?

It's all too much to think about right now. There are so many questions, so many what-if scenarios whipping around my thoughts; my head already feels seconds away from exploding. Between the blood oath, the hunters, Brighton, and Mom's *accident*, I have no idea what to do. I want to run. Desperately. Run until there's no such thing as vampires and hunters and blood oaths. More than that, though, I want to kill Scott Ellis for what he made happen; there is no doubt in my mind he's the reason my mom is lying in a hospital bed right now. He deserves to suffer for what he did; my mom has nothing to do with the vampires, and he went after her to get at me. To *punish* me for being associated with the vampires. As much as the idea of taking one of Brighton's parents from her makes me sick to my stomach, the dark desire I have to see him fall overpowers it.

Without thinking, I pull my phone out of my pocket and tap Brighton's number. The line doesn't ring—it goes straight to voicemail, and I hang up without leaving a message. I can't take the chance of Scott intercepting it, which is why I don't text her either.

Instead, I keep pacing.

My dad comes into the room by the time I've bitten my thumbnail painfully short, holding a paper to-go cup in each hand. He's at least changed his clothes since I arrived yesterday—when I sent him home to have a break—but he looks exhausted. Dark circles under his eyes, messy gray-brown hair, and the wrinkles around his eyes are more pronounced than usual. He appears... frumpy. Which is so incredibly not like him, it worries me.

"You'll wear the tile down to the subfloor if you keep that up, kiddo." The corner of his mouth pulls up slightly, but the smile is forced, and we both know it.

I pause, dropping my hand back to my side. "Yeah."

He walks closer, frowning in what seems to be realization. "Caffeine might not be the best thing for you right now."

He's not wrong; my pulse is already erratic and my thoughts haven't stopped racing since—

"Dad," I blurt in an uneven tone. I can't keep this to myself a second longer. My thoughts are tangled like old Christmas lights, and there's no chance of getting them straight on my own.

He sets both cups on the rolling table at the end of Mom's bed. "What is it, Calla?" He shrugs off his navy rain jacket, draping it over the chair closest to him, then gives me his full attention.

"I…" My voice cuts off. Shaking my head, I clear my throat. "I know you and mom had… um, lost… a baby before I was born."

His brows furrow as his face falls, and he inhales deeply before nodding. "We did. How did you—?"

"I read Mom's medical records," I blurt. I don't feel bad for doing it, considering it's likely the only way I would've ever known about the child they had before me.

"I see," he murmurs in a tired voice. "I'm sorry you found out that way. We should have told you."

"Were you going to?" I ask.

He opens his mouth, then seems to consider what he's going to say. A moment later, he frowns. "It was never a discussion your mom and I had."

Nodding, I say, "So no, then." I steal a glance toward the door before looking back at him. "The baby was a girl." My chest is tight, my throat dry as I force out, "What if this means something? For the oath?"

Dad blinks at me before his eyes widen. "I don't…" He looks over his shoulder at Mom, then back at me. "We shouldn't talk about this right now."

He's probably right. There's no telling who is listening, and the most important thing right now is that Mom gets better. But my head is going to explode if we don't.

"I know it's not the best time or place, but please. I've spent every single day since being told about the oath believing that my future would never be my own. That I wouldn't get to choose what I wanted to be, where I wanted to live... anything. And if that somehow isn't the case—if I *do* get a choice—I want to know. Now."

"I understand, Calla, and you absolutely deserve that. You deserve everything you want out of life, and answers to your questions are the least of what you should get." The sadness in his eyes gives me pause.

"But you don't know, do you?" I ask in a low voice, and he shakes his head after a beat of silence. "You... you never thought to look into it?" There's an edge to my voice, a sliver of hurt in my tone that makes him take a step toward me, but I shift backward.

Dad sighs. "After we lost the baby, your mom and I went through a very difficult period. Her more than me, of course, but I struggled with not knowing how to be there for her in the way she needed. I am sorry to say that trying to figure out what our dead child meant for the oath didn't cross my mind." His eyes are glassy and he turns from me for a moment to wipe the unshed tears away. When he faces me again, he says, "I don't want you to think I'm dismissing this, because I'm not. But I thought once before I was going to lose your mother. Now this happens, and I..." His voice cracks, and he sniffles. "I love you more than life, Calla, but I need to focus on your mom right now. Please try to understand?"

I nod stiffly, because I do understand—I almost lost my mom. "Okay. We can talk about this later."

Later isn't going to be anytime soon, so I go back to pacing.

Dad sits at Mom's bedside, reading yesterday's paper and glancing over at me every few minutes. He sets the paper in his lap and sighs. "Why don't you go for a walk?" he suggests. "Clear your head. Maybe get something to eat?"

I stop pacing and purse my lips. I haven't in a while, and despite all of the upset, I am pretty hungry. My eyes flit to Mom, and I frown, not wanting to leave in case she wakes while I'm gone.

"Calla," Dad says in a soft tone. "Go on. Please."

Finally, I nod. "Call me the second anything changes."

He nods.

Staring at him, I say, "Promise me."

He offers a tired look, setting the paper aside and standing. He walks over to me and touches my cheek in a gesture that's meant to be comforting. As conflicted as my feelings are toward the man who raised me, I don't pull away when he drops his hand and wraps his arms around me. In fact, I hug him back, because despite everything, we're the ones here for Mom and we need to stay strong together—for her.

"I promise, kiddo," he says softly. "Now go." He releases me, kissing the top of my head.

I blink back tears as he appears to do the same, stepping away from me and forcing a watery smile. I do my best to mirror it, then turn and leave the room, sniffling and wiping the wetness that escaped my eyes and fell down my cheeks.

The stark white, obscenely bright hallway makes me squint as I walk across the shiny tile, avoiding the eyes of the nurses and other people passing me going in the opposite direction.

I should step outside and get some air. Or find the cafeteria and pray there's something relatively edible there. I'd even settle for microwaved mac and cheese at this point.

Instead, I head toward the visitor lounge, where the vampires I may or may not be bound to are waiting for me.

3

LEX

The moment Calla walks in, the lot of us stand from the particularly uncomfortable plastic waiting room chairs, and her stride falters. She stays near the doorway, her eyes flicking between us. I haven't seen her this hesitant since the night we showed up at her apartment in Washington, and that was nearly two months ago.

"My dad thought I needed a break," she finally says in a quiet voice. "I guess my pacing was stressing him out," she adds with a half-hearted shrug.

Gabriel moves toward her before any of the rest of us can, touching her cheek gently before wrapping his arms around her. He holds her to him while he smooths his hand over her hair. It's a mess of dark brown waves, which is to be expected given the circumstances, but I think all of us—save maybe for Atlas—are fighting the urge to bring her comfort in any way possible. Kade would probably brush her hair if he wasn't standing silently in the corner of the room. His eyes are on Calla, but they're distant—near-vacant. It makes my stomach twist with unease. There's something more going on there, but I'm not entirely sure how to breach the topic with him.

He lost his sister at the hands of a hunter and watched it happen. Granted their relationship was complicated, but not having the opportunity to change that is clearly eating him up inside.

"How are things going?" I ask after Gabriel pulls back, letting Calla out of his arms but staying close to her side.

She presses her lips together, tilting her head slightly. "You haven't been listening?" Her quiet tone is laced with mild disbelief.

I shake my head. I'd been focusing on some trashy reality show on the flatscreen across the room, figuring whatever was happening between Calla and her parents wasn't my business. I'm not sure I would've taken that same stance even a month ago, but here we are. This scrappy little human has changed all of us, even if we don't want to admit it.

"I was listening," Atlas says in a level voice, and Calla frowns, nodding.

"What are the rest of us missing?" I ask, glancing at Gabriel, who shrugs. Evidently, he wasn't listening either.

Calla lets out a heavy sigh and walks over to one of the chairs, dropping into it before locking eyes with Atlas. "I wasn't the firstborn Montgomery girl."

My eyes go wide and my head whips toward Atlas.

"What?" Kade speaks for the first time since we arrived. His voice is low, gravelly. It makes Calla turn her gaze toward him.

"Uh, yeah." She folds her hands in her lap. "My mom had a baby girl before me. She only lived for a few hours, but..." She trails off, dropping her gaze to her lap.

"The fuck?" I mutter. "What does that mean?"

Gabriel's brows knit as he looks between Calla and Atlas. "It's entirely possible the claim we have to Calla is invalid. The girl we were owed lived; however, not long enough for us to fulfill the blood oath."

"I don't understand any of this," Calla mumbles, "and honestly, I can't think about what it means right now." Her voice cracks and her throat bobs as she swallows, refusing to meet any of our gazes.

Gabriel wraps his arm around her shoulders, pressing a kiss against the side of her head. "We will figure it out later. Right now, you need to focus on being here for your mom."

She clears her throat and nods, then says to no one in particular, "I want whatever security team you had for me looking out for my parents instead. This… this can't happen again."

"Of course," Gabriel assures her. "Fallon and Jase have several trusted friends in the city, and I will contact them personally and ensure things are taken care of."

"Thank you." She sits up straighter, her back pressed into the chair. "I want Scott Ellis dead." Her voice doesn't crack this time, but her eyes are glassy with unshed tears.

The room falls silent for a moment before Kade claps his hands together, a dark look plastered on his face. "Now that's a plan I can get behind," he says, coming over to where the rest of us are standing around Calla.

She blinks, making the tears roll down her cheeks as she nods at Kade. "Good." When Gabriel pulls a handkerchief out of his pocket and holds it down to her, she arches a brow at him. "What's that for?"

He regards her thoughtfully and says in a gentle tone, "Angel, you're crying."

Calla takes the handkerchief and quickly dries her cheeks before handing it back to Gabriel. Her gaze passes over each of us until her phone chimes. She pulls it out, and a look of what I can only describe as a mix of hope and relief fills her face.

"What is it?" Kade asks.

"My mom is awake," Calla says in a thick voice, standing and pocketing her phone. "I—"

"Go," I tell her. "We're not going anywhere."

Her eyes meet mine, and something in my chest feels weirdly pulled toward her. She opens her mouth as if she's going to speak, but then shuts it, opting to nod instead. Without another word, she walks out of the waiting room, leaving a heavy silence in her absence.

Kade scowls, taking the seat Calla left. "Every fucking day it's something new. What the hell are we going to do about this?"

"Perhaps it's worth asking Calla what she *wants* to do about it?" Gabriel offers, raking a hand through his mop of copper hair.

I shove my hands into the pockets of my black jeans and move to lean against the wall next to the doorway. "She's not getting out of this on a technicality." My words are harsh, I'm well aware, but the thought of having Calla walk away from us… I don't want to consider it as a possibility. If that makes me a monster, so be it.

Gabriel offers me a look of understanding but says, "If the oath has no bearing on her, she shouldn't have to—"

"Have to what?" I cut in, irritation prickling at the back of my neck at his words. "Be stuck with us? I think we all know just how much she doesn't hate it, despite what she'd often have us believe."

"It's not as if we're torturing the girl," Kade adds in an absent tone. "Far from it, in fact. She can hardly deny that."

"You'd consider holding her against her will in the absence of a valid agreement?" Gabriel questions, keeping his eyes on Kade, though the words are meant for both of us.

"Do you honestly believe it'd be against her will at this point?" I challenge. "Or, just maybe, we're not giving our girl enough credit. You said it yourself and you're right. Perhaps she *wants* to be with us. Otherwise, what's to keep her from running away? She's still here, isn't she?"

"Her mom is laid up in a hospital bed, for one," Kade says. "You really think she'd take off now?"

My lips press into a thin line for a moment, then I grumble, "Probably not, no."

"Enough," Atlas says, crossing his arms over his chest. "As far as our current problems go, this is the least concerning." His dark expression and sharp tone are clear—this isn't up for discussion at the moment.

"Fine," Kade mutters, "then let's talk about how we're going to deal with the son of a bitch who almost killed Calla's mom."

"I think that's a conversation Calla should be present for," I chime in, "considering from the sounds of it, she'd like to be the one to do it."

"Calla isn't killing anyone," Atlas says, though even he appears rather conflicted about it.

"No?" I offer. "Who are we to deny her that pleasure?" Okay, so *pleasure* might not be exactly the right word in this case, but the anger and hatred in Calla's voice when she told us she wanted Scott dead makes me think her taking him out should be left on the table. And I'll be more than happy to help should she need it.

Atlas sighs, as if I'm testing his patience. "If it's truly what she wants, fine. But you know as well as I do it would feel good for about three seconds, then she'd have to live with the weight of killing someone for the rest of her life."

"Taking a life means something different when you're a vampire," Gabriel says. "I fear it would break her, especially with the target being the father of her best friend."

Kade shrugs. "I say we kill them both."

Atlas pinches the bridge of his nose, shaking his head. "Kade."

I stare at Kade, unsure what to say. Deciding to take out Brighton is a bit extreme, even for us. I can't help but think he wouldn't be so determined to shed blood like this if his sister hadn't just been killed. It isn't an excuse for him lashing out—and I'm sure as hell glad he didn't offer that *suggestion* while Calla was still in the room—but I understand it's coming from a place of pain and trauma, whether he'll admit it or not.

"Oh, come on," Kade continues. "As if you haven't already considered it. That girl is as much of a threat as her father is."

"Calla would disagree," Gabriel says.

"I don't give a fuck, Saint Gabriel," Kade snaps. "It isn't her species at risk, ergo it isn't her call."

"Enough, Kade," Atlas shoots at him. "This is not the place to be having this discussion."

Kade looks as if he wants to argue, but eventually backs down, pressing his lips into a tight line and shaking his head.

My gums throb with discomfort, the hunger clawing at me despite the swirling unease in my stomach. I'm not accustomed to arguing with my brothers, and I feel the overwhelming need to ease the tension between us.

"Anyone else fucking starving?" I ask.

That's something we're in undeniable, eternal agreement over.

✵ 4 ✵
CALLA

My heart pounds in my throat as I all but sprint back to Mom's room. The second I step inside and see her eyes open, mine fill with tears. I rush forward, and surprise flickers across her worn-out expression.

"Calla, what—?"

I have my arms around her, burying my face against her shoulder and the stiff, scratchy material of her hospital gown, before she can finish her sentence.

"Easy, honey," Dad says from where he's sitting in a chair on the other side of the bed.

Squeezing my eyes shut against the tears, I stay there for several seconds longer, then pull back and wipe my cheeks, perching on the edge of the bed. "Sorry. I'm just glad you're okay."

"Me too, sweetheart," she says with a faint smile, reaching for my hands. "You didn't need to come all the way from Washington. I hate to take you away from your studies—I know how important school is to you."

I frown. "Of course I needed to come, Mom." It doesn't

matter that I didn't come here from Washington or that we're essentially on the run from hunters or that the blood oath might be void. All that matters is my mom is alive and she's going to be okay.

"Don't get me wrong, I'm happy to see you, but I'm fine. Just a little accident."

I'm not surprised she's trying to downplay what happened to her. Hell, I'd do it too. It makes thinking about it easier. Which is why I make the choice not to tell either of them the truth—that the *accident* was intentional. The guys will make sure they're protected from here on out, so it won't do any good to reveal Brighton's father was behind the crash. I fight the urge to clench my hands into fists; I can't stop thinking about the phone call I had with Scott before he tried to kill my mom. He will pay for what he did, but it's hard to pretend the thought of taking one of Brighton's parents from her won't hurt like hell.

Revenge is a conflicting desire, and I'm not entirely sure what to do with it right now.

The doctor chooses that moment to pop her head in and check on Mom. She lifts her chart from the holder at the end of the bed and reviews Mom's vitals, checking over the machines, which I think are monitoring her blood pressure and heart rate.

"How's it looking?" Dad asks, reaching mindlessly for Mom's hand. She glances down at the touch and smiles.

"I'm pleased with your improvement," the doctor says to Mom. "I'd like you to stay for a few more days to ensure you remain stable and nothing else comes up, but things are looking quite good at this point."

"Is it really necessary for me to stay?" Mom asks, glancing between Dad and the doctor.

"I'm afraid I must insist on it," she replies with a smile.

I, for one, won't argue on Mom's behalf when it comes to

this. I'd much rather she stay under the supervision of medical staff until they're sure she's completely fine.

"Don't worry, dear," Dad says to her, "you'll be home before you know it, and I'll be here with you until you're ready to leave."

She sighs, sneaking a glance at me, and I nod in agreement with the others. "All right, fine," she says finally. "Can I at least get a proper meal?"

Dad laughs. "Whatever you want, it's yours."

The doctor slips out of the room, and I can't help but smile watching my parents. Despite the years of resentment I held for my father, for what he kept secret, seeing him with Mom is a reminder that he's a good man. He loves us, regardless of the blood oath he neglected to share with his wife before she became pregnant with his child. And now... well, now it may not even matter.

"Honey," Mom says, pulling my attention back to her. "I do appreciate you being here, but I'm sure you need to get back to Washington and study for finals."

I don't bother telling her that I've been out of school for a while. Unfortunately, it's pretty close to the bottom of my list of problems at the moment. And as much as I don't want to leave my mom here like this, it's not safe to stay in NYC. The hunters will know I'm here and likely assume the guys are with me, which pretty much makes them sitting ducks... er, vampires. Whatever.

Concern for their safety wasn't anything I thought would even be on my radar, but there's an uncomfortable tension in my chest that proves it very much is. I would be wrecked if any of them were hurt—or worse—because they were here to support me.

Do I have any idea what's going to happen? No.

If the blood oath is in fact void and I am, for all intents and purposes, free of Atlas, Lex, Kade, and Gabriel, what will happen? I have no freaking clue, and the thought alone makes my pulse race and my palms sweat. We'll have to face it eventually, but given the choice to stay with the guys or explore the future I never thought I'd have… I'm not sure what I'll do.

"I don't want to leave you," I tell Mom in a low voice, my throat thick with emotion I'm struggling to hold back.

"I'm okay, Calla," she assures me. "I'll get out of here in a few days, and your father will take care of me at home."

I hold her gaze for several seconds, then finally, I sigh in defeat. "Okay." I reach for her hand and give it a gentle squeeze before looking across the bed at my dad. "I'll go back on the condition that you keep me up to speed with every-thing happening here. I want to be updated at least three times daily and—"

Mom laughs, cutting off my tirade. "Honey, relax. We will make sure you know what's going on, but please don't worry about me. You heard what the doctor said. I'm okay." Her voice is gentle but firm.

I give her a hug, hanging on a little longer than normal, and kiss her cheek. "Call me if you need anything, okay? Please?"

She presses her hand against my cheek, smiling at me. "Sure. Take care of yourself, Calla. I love you."

I blink back the sudden rush of tears and nod. "I love you," I echo.

After another extended hug, Dad walks me to the door, where we share a hug as well.

"Keep me posted," I tell him, sniffling as I glance at Mom over his shoulder. Her eyes are closed again, the machines around her beeping steadily.

"Calla, I—" His voice cracks. "Stay."

My brows shoot up, and I shake my head. "What? Dad—"

"You don't have to go with them," he says in a hard voice.

"We'll figure out the blood oath. This could be your way out. You don't have to go back to Washington. We can have you transferred to NYU to finish your degree. You can live at home or we can get you an apartment in the city—whatever you want."

I don't bother telling him that I'm not going back to Washington. That would require a much longer conversation about the hunters that I don't have the mental capacity to have at the moment.

Instead of addressing his offer, I ask, "Are you going to tell Mom that I found out about the baby?"

"Yes. Stay, and when she's better, we can tell her together. I never thought we'd have a chance to save you from those monsters, but this… If the oath was technically fulfilled by your sister the moment she was born, it was never your burden to bear, Calla. I am so sorry you've had to live with it as long as you have and that I never considered this before."

"It's not that simple, Dad. This is a potential loophole to the oath, sure, but…" I trail off, not sure how to explain to my dad how I've come to care about the vampires who took me from my apartment—my life—two months ago.

His face falls, and he reaches for my hands, holding them in his against his chest. "Please, Calla. I know this is scary, but if it means your freedom, we need to at least try."

I press my lips together, willing my chin to stop trembling. "There's more to it than you know. I'm sorry, Dad. I don't know how to explain everything to you right now, but there's far more at stake at the moment. I… I have to go." I swallow the lump in my throat, pulling my hands back before wrapping them around my dad in a quick, tight hug. I kiss his cheek, then turn and walk away without looking back.

C alla is silent the entire drive from the hospital to the hotel Gabriel reserved a suite at. Understandable, of course, but not something I'm used to. I decide quite quickly that I don't like it. I much prefer her sharp tongue and wit. It was clear when she returned to the waiting room and announced she was ready to leave that she didn't truly want to, but none of us questioned her or mentioned the conversation we all overheard between Calla and her father. Of course he wanted to save her from us, that much wasn't surprising in the least. What did confound me was her response. It was almost as if she wasn't sure she *wanted* to be free of us. I sure as hell don't want to let her go, voided blood oath be damned.

Once we've checked in at the hotel and settled into the penthouse suite, Kade disappears into the bathroom, the shower turning on a moment later. Gabriel and Atlas sit in deep blue armchairs across from each other in the living room, and Calla busies herself making tea in the full kitchen on the far side of the suite, keeping her back to us.

I fight the urge to go to her, knowing she probably needs

some space to figure things out. That does nothing to appease the monster in me that wants to devour her. My cock twitches, and I groan inwardly, considering joining Kade in the shower, but he seems even less approachable as of late. Looks like I'll just have to deal with the hard-on I'm sporting until I can deal with it myself. In the meantime, I distract myself by listening to the steady beat of Calla's heart from across the room. I never expected something so mundane to be so calming, but I suppose there are a lot of things about the human in our midst I never could have expected.

When Kade reappears from the bathroom, his hair damp and smelling of aftershave and mouthwash, the five of us sit down together.

Calla folds her legs under her and sips her tea before looking at each of us. "We need to talk about the oath. Whether or not it's void, I think we all know we're bound in ways that have nothing to do with the agreement my ancestor made with you." She sets the steaming mug on the small, marble side table in between her chair and mine. "I'd like to make contact with the witch Selene sent to undo that blood spell. Maybe she knows more about the oath and can provide a definitive answer to its validity."

"I will track her down," Gabriel offers.

Calla nods, then a moment later sighs. "Something I don't understand is your ability to track me. Clearly, we're still connected in some way, which makes me think the oath could be valid."

"Not necessarily," Atlas says. "There's a bond between us, yes, but that may not mean what we've believed it to mean. We are connected to your blood, that much is true. Because you are born into the Montgomery line, we can sense you as I'm sure you could sense us given the proper training and time."

She blinks at him, her pulse ticking faster beneath her skin. "What does that mean?"

"It means we're connected, but it's possible that because you're not technically the firstborn daughter since the blood oath was entered into, *your* life isn't promised to us," Gabriel answers. "We have been connected to every Montgomery born since the agreement was made. The bonds were never incredibly strong—nothing like that of a vampire and their sire, for instance—but they were there. Each time a Montgomery child was born, we would have to check if it was a girl, and when it wasn't, we'd learn to ignore the bond until it faded completely."

She falls silent, dropping her chin slightly as her shoulders slump. "What about the girl born before me?"

I rub my jaw, leaning my elbow on the armrest of my chair. "We felt the bond snap into place when the child was born, but it broke so quickly, we didn't have a chance to check if it had been a girl. Your mom wasn't the first to lose a Montgomery child, but the others were lost much earlier on."

Calla's shoulders move as she sighs, picking at a loose thread on her shirt before she lifts her head to look at me. "You didn't bother to check this one?"

I shake my head. "It happened during a time where things between the vampires and hunters were... much like they are now. We had more immediate concerns."

She nods, but her gaze is nearly vacant, caught somewhere between shock and loss. "Okay," she finally says, flattening her hands on her thighs.

"Okay?" I ask, searching her face.

Calla shrugs. "What do you want me to say? What's done is done, and none of us can change the past. Right now, I think the most important thing for us to do is focus on the future. Things aren't exactly sunshine and rainbows, remember? We need to make a plan." She goes to stand, but Gabriel stops her.

"Slow down, angel. We don't need to do anything right this second."

"We shouldn't waste any time," she tells him, shifting her gaze toward Kade, then Atlas. "You know it as well, if not better, than I do."

"Perhaps," Gabriel continues, "but we also need to take care of each other. You should eat something and get some rest."

"Our problems aren't going anywhere," I add, echoing Gabriel's concern for Calla—and the rest of us. "They will still be problems tomorrow."

She pulls her bottom lip between her teeth, seemingly considering our words. My gaze gets stuck on her mouth, and the desire to reach for her, to taste her lips, nearly over-takes my control.

"Lex," Gabriel says in a firm voice, eyeing me sternly from beside her.

I shrug, my lips curling into a grin. "Sorry?"

Calla rolls her eyes, a tinge of pink filling her cheeks under my stare. "You are not."

My grin widens. "Yeah, I'm not." I stand, offering her my hand. "I think it's time we let ourselves forget about the day, enjoy each other's company, and—"

"Get naked?" Kade offers, flashing a bit of fang.

"Preferably," I answer, shooting Calla a wink.

She eyes my outstretched hand, and her pulse ticks faster as she slowly reaches for it, placing her palm against mine before standing from the chair.

I guide her toward the king-size bed across the room as Kade and Gabriel trail behind us. Pulling back the heavy duvet with one hand, I keep my other wrapped around Calla's. Then, without warning, I scoop her up, surprised when she instantly wraps her legs around my waist. "That a girl," I murmur, dropping my mouth to her collarbone. Her skin is flushed and warm, and it shoots right to my cock, making it throb with the need to take her.

She drags her tongue along my bottom lip before pushing it into my mouth, deepening the kiss as she buries her fingers in my hair.

I barely hear the sound of Atlas growling across the room over the sound of Calla's pounding heartbeat. I fucking love that I can get her going this easily.

Gabriel and Kade move around us, sliding into the bed, while I lay her in between them, breaking the kiss for a brief moment before Gabriel takes my place, capturing her chin and tilting her face toward him. Their lips meet, and I step back to tug my shirt off, dropping it onto the dark stained hardwood as Atlas stalks toward us, his gaze dark and hungry.

I make quick work of losing my pants, catching Kade's gaze as I turn back to the bed. Something in his eyes calls to me, and I'm moving before I even realize what I'm doing. My hands close around the hem of his shirt, and I pull it over his head. I enjoy the view of his thick, toned muscles, dragging my gaze down his chest toward the dark hair leading to the waistband of his jeans. I unbuckle his belt as Atlas moves beside me, catching Calla's attention. Her eyes widen slightly, taking in the situation, and her heart races. Her bare chest is flushed, and Gabriel unclasps her bra, freeing her breasts and quickly dropping his mouth to them, kissing and sucking, filling the room with the sound of Calla's short breaths and moans.

It's a good thing our suite came with a massive bed, because in a matter of minutes, all five of us are piled into it.

Atlas slowly pulls Calla's pants down to her ankles, and she shivers, her skin covered in goosebumps. She holds her breath as he pulls off his shirt and lowers himself between her thighs, burying his face there, and if that sight isn't enough to set me off, nothing is.

I slide my hand into Kade's boxers and free his hard cock, pumping my hand up and down its length as my gaze bounces between him and what Atlas and Gabriel are doing to elicit the most delicious moans from our girl.

"Fuck," he grunts, gripping the sheets on either side of him. His hand finds Calla's, and their fingers intertwine. Kade's head falls back against the pillow and his eyes close as he bites his lip, thrusting his hips up. I alternate speed and the tightness of my grip, moving at a speed no human could match and making his breath come faster. He opens his eyes and lifts the hand that's holding Calla's, offering me her wrist. I don't hesitate—at that moment, I can't. My fangs extend to their full length, and I sink them into Calla's wrist, groaning as her hot, sweet blood explodes over my tastebuds. It fills my gut with warmth and my dick gets even harder. I close my eyes, reveling in the spark of energy zipping through my veins as I continue pumping Kade's cock. I pull away from Calla's wrist when I've had enough, opening my eyes as Kade guides their intertwined hands back to the mattress, leaning over to lick the wound shut. I reach down and cup his balls in my free hand, massaging them in time with my movements along his throbbing shaft. His jaw is clenched so tight it looks sharp enough to cut glass, and his eyes fly up to meet mine. My breath stills at the darkness there, despite the way he's moaning as I work my hand over his cock.

"Kade—"

"Shut up," he growls. "Don't fucking stop."

Atlas peers over Calla's thigh at us, arching a brow for a brief moment before returning to his ministrations, making her cry out as he devours her pussy with his mouth. Gabriel seals his lips over hers, kissing her deeply, muffling the sound, and rolls her nipple between his fingers. Her back arches, her hips vaulting off the bed, and Atlas quickly traps them against the mattress, fucking her pussy with his tongue until she's trembling, coming hard against his mouth while Gabriel devours hers. Atlas licks her clean before standing and moving behind me, capturing my attention. He nods toward Calla, then smoothly takes over pumping Kade's cock as I shift over, quickly removing my pants and boxers, freeing my wicked erection.

Calla's eyes widen, bouncing between my cock and my face, and I can't help but grin as I run my hand along my thick length. I take note of the bulge in Gabriel's pants and nod at him before turning my full attention to Calla and the beautiful blush in her cheeks. I lean down, placing a soft kiss against her lips but pulling back before she can respond. "Tell me," I murmur, my lips tracing the shell of her ear, "would you like Gabriel to fuck that gorgeous ass of yours while I bury my cock in your pussy?" I press another chaste kiss against her lips, then move to her other ear. "Or shall I be granted the pleasure of stretching you there?"

"Fucking hell," she mutters breathlessly.

I tut my tongue, meeting her gaze. "That's not an answer, Calla."

Her eyes are narrowed but filled with arousal. "I don't care, just fuck me."

I run the blunt head of my cock along her folds, adding pressure when I reach her clit and making her suck in a sharp breath. "So demanding," I purr as Gabriel shifts off the bed and removes his pants and boxers, his cock hard and thick. I lick my lips, turning my gaze back to Calla. "I've been thinking about burying myself between your lovely thighs for too long now." I move without warning and at a speed too fast for her to track. In the time it takes her to blink, I've grabbed her and maneuvered myself under her. She yelps in surprise, which very quickly morphs into a moan when I grab her hips, lining my cock up with her entrance, and sink inside her, stretching her tight walls. I groan as she squeezes me, her head thrown back, pushing her breasts out toward my face. The bed shifts as Gabriel moves behind her, and I catch the hot as fuck sight of him running his hand along his shaft as he gets ready, lubing himself up before rubbing Calla's back. She's still managing to hold herself up as I thrust in and out of her pussy, but something tells me once Gabriel pushes into her, she won't be able to for long.

Her eyes widen and her heart races when Gabriel settles behind her. She bites her lip, her gaze locked on mine, and a sliver of panic flickers across her face.

"Relax," I murmur. "Keep your eyes on me and just breathe."

Gabriel's hands slide over her hips, and I keep still inside her pussy. "Angel?" Gabriel checks in a velvet-soft voice.

Her eyes flick between mine. "I'm okay." She takes a deep breath.

I nod in encouragement. "Good girl. Just like that."

Gabriel pushes his cock into her ass slowly, and she tenses.

"Fuck," she hisses, collapsing on top of me, pushing my cock in deeper.

"Shh," Gabriel murmurs, leaning over her to kiss the skin below her ear. He gives her a minute to adjust to him, stroking her back soothingly. "I'm going to go deeper now."

I reach between us and find her clit, circling it with my thumb as I continue holding still inside her, which is one of the fucking hardest things I've done in my many years on this earth when all I want to do is pound her pussy until my release fills the deepest parts of her.

Slowly, her muscles start to unclench and she begins to relax.

"That's it," I murmur. "Take a deep breath for me now."

Just as she does, Gabriel pushes the rest of the way into her, so we're filling her completely.

"Keep breathing, angel," Gabriel says in a thick voice. He's holding back as well.

"I'm… trying." Her cheeks are flushed and her chest rises and falls quickly with each breath.

"You're doing so well," I tell her, circling her clit faster as I lean up to seal my mouth over hers. She kisses me back, moaning against my lips as Gabriel starts to pull back before pushing in deeper. The movement stimulates her pussy, and she clenches around me. I thrust my hips up, tilting my head to deepen the kiss, and the three of us find a steady rhythm in a matter of thrusts, while Atlas continues working his hand over Kade's cock.

Calla pulls her mouth away from mine, crying out as her muscles tense, squeezing both Gabriel and me. Pressure builds low in my stomach, and we're both thrusting into her at an inhuman speed, vaulting us all over the edge. The room fills with the sounds of our combined orgasms—deep moans and near-animalistic grunts.

Gabriel pulls out of Calla's ass, collapsing into the chair against the wall next to the bed to catch his breath, and Calla falls onto the bed next to me as I slide out of her pussy.

Kade grunts deeply on my other side, and I turn to watch as Calla's lips press along my collarbone. A few more firm, quick pumps and he finds his release, groaning loudly despite trying to press his lips shut to muffle the sound. He slides out from under Atlas and gets off the bed before any of us can reach for him. A moment later, the door to the bathroom slams shut, and Calla flinches next to me. I glance down at her, and she's already looking at me.

"He's not—" she starts.

"I know," I say with a sigh.

"What can we do?" she asks in a small, tired voice.

"I think we should give him time and space," Gabriel answers from her other side.

"I'm worried about him."

I slide my hand into hers and give it a squeeze. "Me too, but it'll be all right."

"I... okay," she finally says. A moment later, her stomach rumbles loud enough, we don't need vampire senses to hear it.

Atlas glances over at us from where he's standing at the end of the bed. "Room service it is," he says, walking into the living room and picking up the hotel phone to call down to the kitchen.

I push my hearing out, trying to focus on Kade, but all I can hear is his breathing. It's still a bit fast, but it's evening out. The heavy pit of concern in my stomach grows bigger still. Gabriel's right—he needs time and space. But I can't help but worry if we give him too much, we could lose him.

Half an hour later, we're sitting around the living room in different stages of undress, watching some ridiculous rom-com Calla picked out and stuffing our faces with a variety of deep fried foods.

Despite the war raging on between the vampires and hunters outside this hotel room, it's dangerously easy to sit here—with my arm around Calla's waist and her head resting on my shoulder as she drifts off to sleep—and pretend this moment of peace is real. That it's something we can have long-term.

I'm not naive by any means, but fuck if I don't want it to last.

❦ 6 ❦

CALLA

For the briefest of moments when I wake the next morning, my thoughts aren't plagued with vampire wars and blood oaths. There are a few short minutes of peace where all I think about is the feel of Atlas's tongue devouring me, or Lex's cock buried deep in my pussy, or Gabriel's in my ass, until nothing else but them exist in my world.

A sigh escapes my lips, and without opening my eyes, I reach out... only to find the massive bed empty.

I yawn, rubbing my eyes as I prop myself up on my elbows. Sunlight fills the room, making it look even fancier, if that's possible. The crisp white sheets and soft gray walls are simple yet elegant. As is the silver and crystal chandelier that hangs over the bed from the vaulted ceiling. The sliding frosted glass door that divides the bedroom from the rest of the suite is closed over almost completely, but the sound of the guys' muffled voices reaches me from the other room.

They're talking quietly, but I can hear the sharp anger in Atlas's voice. Gabriel seems to be the one offering calm responses to whatever is being said, which doesn't surprise me, considering he's always been the calm in the storm when it comes to them—at least in my experience.

I stretch my legs out and push the duvet off before swinging them over the side of the bed. I wrap the bedsheet around me and walk out to the living room to see what's going on, the soft white material trailing behind me like a gown.

The guys stop talking and turn their attention toward me the moment they sense me there, and Gabriel stands, walking toward me as he rakes a hand through his messy copper hair.

"Good morning, angel," he greets in a soft voice, smiling at me. His chest is bare, and my eyes immediately drop to the tight muscles there, inching even lower to the black trousers he's wearing dangerously low on his hips. His voice nudges my attention back upward. "Are you hungry? We can have room service brought up, and there's a French press on the counter that's fresh."

"I'm not hungry," I tell him, swallowing hard and forcing myself to refocus. "What's going on?" When none of them answer my question, I fold my arms over my chest as best as I can while still covering myself with the bedsheet and sigh. "I'm not going to take silence as an answer this time. Tell me what's going on. You guys stopped talking the second I walked into the room."

"I, for one, was distracted by the mere thought of your naked body under that sheet," Lex says with a wicked smirk that sends heat through me despite my irritation at them for being annoyingly unforthcoming. I should be used to it by now, but I thought we'd turned over a new leaf, so why are they hiding something from me now?

"Yeah?" I say, playing into his words. "Tell me what you were talking about, and maybe I'll give you a better look." I'm entirely not serious, but Lex seems to consider it, while Atlas and Kade exchange a brief look, and Gabriel doesn't take his eyes off me.

Atlas clears his throat, snagging my attention. He's the only one of the group fully dressed, wearing dark gray slacks, a black V-neck, and a leather jacket, with his hair combed back. The others are in various stages of undress—Lex's white hair is slicked back and still wet from a shower, but he's wearing jeans and shoes, though no shirt. Kade has clearly not showered. His hair is a mess and he's wearing nothing but a pair of black boxer shorts. The dark circles under his eyes make my chest ache for him, and I have an awful feeling whatever situation I've just walked into is going to make that ache much more painful.

"There was another attack against the hunters about four hours ago," Atlas says. "I didn't know it was happening until it was already underway."

My eyes widen and my grip on the bedsheet tightens. "Another attack so soon? Why?"

"The vampires who orchestrated it didn't want to give the hunters a chance to recover from the initial attack."

My stomach drops in the same moment my heart leaps into my throat. "Was Scott killed?" That should have been my first question, though I'm not sure if I'll be happy about it or resentful that I didn't have the opportunity to strike him down myself. I shudder at the heavy sensation that grips me. I'm thinking about killing another human being. Despite the awful things he's done, I'm terrified of what these violent urges might suggest about me.

Atlas shakes his head. "No, he wasn't. However, Brighton's mother was. Scott had been checking in on her and Brighton when it happened. There was a group of vampires tailing him, and he managed to escape, but unfortunately she did not."

Tears fill my eyes, and I shake my head, backing away

regardless of the devastating knowledge that I have nowhere to go. *Because nowhere is safe even under the protection of four vampires.*

"Brighton?" I force out, and my voice cracks.

"She's fine," Kade chimes in without looking at me. His bare feet are propped on the armrest of the couch where he's lounging, staring at the ceiling. "She wasn't with them when the attack happened."

But she easily could have been.

I immediately feel the urge to go to Brighton, to be there for my best friend—to comfort and protect her. Panic consumes me, pressing on my chest so hard I can't breathe. I try to swallow past the dryness in my throat, but it does little to help the feeling of suffocating. My head swims as dizziness floods through me and each breath becomes harder than the last. I can't think straight. Too much is happening.

Gabriel reaches for me, and I reel back, my vision blurry with tears.

Lex stands, as if he too is going to come toward me, his brows drawn together in concern. "Calla—"

"No," I croak. "This isn't... I can't..." My chest heaves as my breaths come in short gasps. *I can't breathe.*

Before I know what's happening, my legs give out. Gabriel catches me around my waist before I hit the floor, holding me against his chest.

The room tilts around me, darkening as the sounds around me start to fade in and out, echoing through me.

"Look at me, angel." Gabriel's voice somehow slices through my hysteria, and the moment our eyes meet, I am grounded. "Breathe," he says in a voice that leaves no room for anything but compliance. The power of his influence settles over me like a warm, weighted blanket, filling me with comfort and steadiness—enough to allow me a moment to catch my breath. At that moment, I can't even contemplate attempting to resist the vampire's glamour—I don't *want* to. He can pull me out of this never-ending fall I'm experiencing, and I'm desperate enough not to fight him.

I inhale deeply, holding his gaze as he nods in encouragement, then let the breath out slowly, finding I'm able to stand again. My legs are still a bit unsteady, but with Gabriel holding me, I'm not worried about ending up on the floor.

"There you go," he murmurs. "Stay with me and keep breathing slowly." His fingers splay across my cheek, warming my skin as my pulse slowly returns to a normal pace.

"She good?" Lex asks from somewhere behind Gabriel.

"She's just fine," he answers without breaking eye contact with me, and I find myself nodding.

"I'm better now," I say in a low voice.

Gabriel nods, then pulls his gaze from mine, severing the glamour, but makes no move to shift away from me.

I turn my face and press my lips to his palm in a soft kiss. "Thank you," I whisper. I wasn't prepared for the moment where I would thank a vampire for glamouring me, but here we are.

Glancing past Gabriel, it appears that Lex and Kade slipped out of the room. Something tells me—and I hope—they might have gone for breakfast for me and blood for them.

Atlas lingers, always in the background, always watching. His silver eyes are focused, but I can see the exhaustion behind his sharp facade.

I slip into the bedroom and put yesterday's clothes back on before returning to the living room, where Atlas and Gabriel are drinking coffee on the couch.

"I have no idea what I'm supposed to do now. I still want to kill Scott for what he did to my mom, but how can I be okay with taking Brighton's only living parent from her?"

Atlas sets his mug on the table and says in a flat voice, "That's not your call. Scott will die either way."

"So what you're saying is you're going to kill him?" I ask.

"Well, Lex seems to think we should leave that pleasure to you. If you're not too emotional to handle it."

My stomach drops at his tone. It's devoid of any true emotion and it rubs me in all the wrong places. "Do you expect me to be…? What, like you? Of course I'm going to be emotional about it. This is my best friend's father, not just some random hunter. Brighton already lost one parent. *I* almost did too. You expect me to be okay with this?"

Atlas's sharp eyes flick between mine, missing the pain I'm sure is filling my own gaze. "I'm not saying you have to do it, Calla. I'm saying if that's what you *want*, the kill is yours."

We stare at each other for a moment. I swallow past the emotion building in my chest, then open my mouth to respond, but nothing comes out.

The worst part? Atlas is right. Scott needs to die—and that's going to break Brighton.

I flee the room without another word. I don't know what to say at this point. My throat is thick with unshed tears, and I turn on the shower as if that will cover the sound of the sob clawing its way up my throat. I pull my phone out of my back pocket and dial Brighton's number. The line doesn't even ring once before I get an automated message that says, "We're sorry. The number you have reached has been disconnected or is no longer in service."

The phone slips from my hand, clattering against the white marble vanity as I stare at my reflection in the mirror. It's one with bright lighting all around it, which really doesn't help the washed-out and splotchy look of my face.

I turn on the cold water and splash my face, pressing my fingers to my temples as wetness trails down my cheeks, dripping onto the front of my shirt. I look into the mirror as if my reflection is going to tell me what to do, how to survive this and get through it unscathed. A voice in the back of my head, low and cruel, tells me I won't. I won't make it through this without loss, whether it be one of the vampires I've come to care for, my family, or my best friend.

In this world, no one makes it out alive—even if they're meant to be immortal.

7

LEX

Walking the streets of New York City makes me reminiscent of the days I lived in Brooklyn and spent much of my time in the city. Of the nights I spent going from bar to bar with friends after long days in the office, meeting women I never knew the names of —nor saw more than once. On occasion, maybe twice.

Walking this path with Kade now, heading toward a blood bank, where Marcel assured us the staff would be accommodating and supply us with blood during our stay in the city, I can't help but worry about the vampire beside me. Even last night, with my hand wrapped around his cock, he was distant, and he seems to be growing more so every day. None of us expect him to be okay, to bounce back to normal after watching his sister who he just reconnected with be killed by hunters, but I refuse to let him suffer in silence. If the roles were reversed, he'd be the same way with any of us.

We pass a couple slow walkers and round the corner to a less busy street lined by red brick row houses, and I punch him in the shoulder, firm but lighthearted. "You can talk to me, you know." I'm not sure how else to breach the subject and get a conversation going. In the decades I've known Kade, I've never seen him like this, which makes me wary on how to approach the matter.

He huffs out a humorless laugh, keeping stride next to me. "About what?"

I shoot him a sideways look, shrugging with my hands in my jacket pockets. "So we're just going to pretend that you're totally fine and not being super weird, even for you?"

It's Kade's turn to shrug. "No idea what you're talking about." It takes him a moment to realize I've stopped walking, and he turns around, arching a brow at me. "What?" he asks.

"You know what," I tell him. "You're not okay. We all know it. We all see it every single day and none of us know what the fuck we're supposed to do to help you."

He glances skyward, his shoulders rising and falling with a sigh. "There's nothing for you to do, Lex. I don't know what you want me to tell you. This is me. Living with what happened. And the moment I get my hands on any one of those hunters, I'm going to shred them to ribbons." His fangs are fully extended by the time he finishes speaking, and I take a quick glance around to make sure we're not being watched.

I blow out a breath. "Yeah, that's all fine and good, but I'm worried about you. We all are."

"No thanks," Kade says plainly, pursing his lips as he shoves his hands into his pockets and rocks back on his heels.

I step toward him. "The fuck? What do you mean, *no thanks?*"

He blinks at me. "I don't want your worry. It's useless to me."

I grab the front of his leather jacket and pull him off the street, hauling him into an alley between two concrete buildings, and slam him against the solid wall. "You need to get your shit together and talk to us, brother. I understand everything with the hunters was bad and you need time to heal from the loss of—"

Kade growls, cutting me off. "What I need, *brother*, is to kill some hunters."

I don't let him go. In fact, I tighten my grip on his jacket, leaning in so close our heavy breaths are mixing. "I understand. Whatever you've got going on in your head, it isn't your burden to face alone. We're here for you. You're my brother, as much as Gabriel and Atlas are. We are a family, however dysfunctional we are sometimes, so don't block us out now. We've been through so much shit together. Don't let this be what comes between us. I want them dead as much as you do. I swear, I will make it happen. These attacks will only continue and we will make sure the hunters fall."

Something in Kade's gaze wavers, and he swallows hard, his jaw clenched tightly. He drops his cheek to my shoulder, letting out a shuddering breath, and we stand there for a moment.

I inhale deeply, closing my eyes at the crisp, clean scent of him, and press my lips together. His lips brush my throat, and my heart races, my pulse zipping with energy. I tip my head to the side slightly, licking my lips, and whisper, "Go ahead." My heart beats faster and my dick hardens.

There's a brief moment of hesitation before Kade sinks his fangs into my neck.

I gasp softly, pulling in a slow breath as my blood flows freely into his mouth, and he groans against me, palming the front of my pants while he feeds. My blood won't give him much sustenance. Maybe a bit from the last human blood I had, which is typically why vampires don't feed off each other, but it does bond us in a way that some would be uncomfortable with.

Kade and I—we've always had a deep level of under-standing for each other, being able to give the other what they needed, even knowing what they needed before they knew it. It's something I'm not prepared to lose. I'm going to do whatever it takes to get the Kade I know back, to save him from the demons I know are trying to control him. Because I've felt them too.

I push against him, desperate for the friction he's creating between my legs, and when he shoves his hand past the waistband of my pants and wraps his hand around my throb-bing cock, I growl a curse at him.

His fangs retract, and he laps at my neck while moving his hand up and down my length before pulling it out of my pants to give him better access. He grabs my shoulder and turns us around so I'm against the wall now. I lean against it, tipping my head back as Kade pumps his hand faster, alter-nating speed and pressure enough to drive me fucking wild. My blood stains his lips and my gaze flicks to his eyes, but he's staring at my cock, his pulse pounding just as hard as mine.

"Fuck," I groan through my teeth, warmth spreading through me as if I had been the one to feed. "You're going to make me come." The muscles in my stomach clench and the tip of my cock glistens with moisture, but Kade's movements don't slow. In fact, he works me harder, faster, until my breath hitches and my muscles coil tight. I grunt, spilling my release onto Kade's hand.

"Feel better?" he asks, a hint of a smirk on his lips as he kneels, cleaning his hand in a puddle of rainwater.

I tuck myself back into my pants and arch a brow at him. "I was going to ask you the same thing."

He straightens, offering me a one-shouldered shrug. "Distractions help, I guess, but the anger I've felt since Meredith… it doesn't go away, Lex. It ebbs and flows, and when it's at its greatest height, I'm worried about what I could do."

I nod in understanding, then ask, "To us?"

"Calla mostly," he admits. "The rest of you can protect yourselves."

"Yes, and we'll protect her too." I shake my head. "Kade, you're not going to hurt Calla."

"No more than we already have, you mean," he comments in a low voice.

The warmth in me is quickly washed away. "We've done some shitty things, yeah, but I think we all can tell how different things have become. We care about the fiery little human, and I can say with some confidence that she cares for us as well."

"What do you think she'll do once we figure out if the oath is valid?"

A heavy pit of unease unfurls in my stomach, and I shake my head again. "I have no fucking clue."

"You want her to stay as much as I do," he says.

"I do," I answer without hesitation.

Do we deserve her? Abso-fucking-lutely not.

But she has become part of us, and it'll be a cold day in hell before any of us let her go without a fight.

That being said, if we find out Calla wasn't meant to be ours, and she decides to leave, we'll have to set her free. But I hope—more than I'd care to admit—she *chooses* to stay.

8

CALLA

I sit on the shiny white marble floor of the bathroom, scrolling through old photos of Brighton and me, knowing it's not going to make me feel any better but unable to stop myself from doing it. Will looking at pictures from the spring break we spent in Mexico bring her mom back or stop the vampires and hunters from killing each other? Of course not, but it's sure as hell a decent, albeit short-lived, distraction.

After half an hour, I force myself up from the heated tile and am walking toward the bathroom door when my phone chimes with a text message from an unknown number.

My heart beats faster as I read the message.

Hey, it's Tessa. We met a while ago when I reversed the magic in your blood. Gabriel reached out and said that you wanted to talk. What's up?

I chew my bottom lip, staring at the message, unsure how to reply to that. When I met Tessa back in Washington, she seemed like someone that I could be friends with, so I feel a little bad reaching out to her now when I need something.

I type out several responses before landing on one, short and sweet.

I have questions I'm hoping you can answer.

Her response comes a few seconds later.

I'll do my best. Where and when can we meet?

I'll have to check, I type back, *but the sooner the better*. I need to figure out what the hell is going on with this blood oath, what it means, and also about my newfound ability to resist glamour. And at this point, if I don't get answers soon, I'm going to lose my damn mind.

Let me know when and where, and I'll be there, she says.

One last look in the mirror, and I take a deep breath, running my fingers through my hair to fix the mess it has become, and walk back to the other room.

Atlas and Gabriel are still in the sitting area. Atlas is on his phone and Gabriel is sipping from a cup of coffee.

I pocket my phone and approach them. "How long are we going to stay in New York City? I heard from Tessa, and we're trying to make plans to meet up."

"We'll be here until we get more information from our contacts in Washington on the latest attack," Atlas says.

"I'll take you to see Tessa," Gabriel chimes in. "I know you want answers and from what I know of Tessa, I believe we can trust her, at least with this."

I pull my phone back out and let Tessa know we're still in New York City. She responds a minute later, saying that she needs some time to deal with things on her end but can fly here in a couple of days to meet us. We agree she'll let us know when she arrives and leave it there for now.

I drop onto the couch next to Gabriel and sigh. "I'm worried about Brighton. I tried calling her but her phone was disconnected, which I assume we have Scott to thank for. I want her kept safe. Is there any way someone in Washington can figure out what's going on? And maybe bring her here?"

"No," Atlas cuts in. "We're not going to lead the hunters directly to us."

I don't miss a beat in my response. "Brighton isn't a hunter."

Atlas just shakes his head without looking up from his phone.

"I just want to know that my best friend is alive." I choke on the words, pulling back when Gabriel tries to reach for me.

"I'll get in touch with her," he assures me, "but that's the best I can do right now."

As scared and as angry as I am, I do know that, but I also know I can't just sit here doing nothing.

I get off the couch and find my shoes, lacing them up. Figuring this hotel is fancy enough, they should have a gym, and I need something to keep my mind occupied.

"Where are you going?" Gabriel asks, but before I can answer, Atlas stands, setting his phone on the table. "I'll go with you," he says as if he read my mind and knew I was planning to go searching for the gym.

I didn't exactly want company, but if Atlas is anywhere near as conflicted as I am with what's going on, I understand the need for the distraction, so I don't argue.

We head there together, and I frown when we step inside the bright, open room and I realize there are a few people already working out, one woman jogging on the treadmill and one guy spotting another on the bench press in front of a wall of floor to ceiling windows overlooking Central Park.

Without hesitation, Atlas uses vampire speed to appear before each person, glamouring them to leave the gym. I walk further into the room as they head for the door without acknowledging me. Once they're gone, Atlas locks the set of frosted glass double doors and prowls closer to me. Despite the cold air being blown into the space, a flush spreads across my chest under his predatory gaze.

I arch a brow at him as the room seems to get smaller, then shift back a few steps, bumping into a mini fridge stocked with towels and water bottles. My eyes snap back to Atlas, who continues closing the distance between us at an unhurried pace. "What… are you doing?"

"You wanted a distraction," he answers simply.

"Yeah, well, so did you. That's why we're here."

"Exactly," he says, the corner of his mouth quirking ever so slightly.

"I was going to run on the treadmill or lift weights. I don't know what you're doing," I tell him, propping my hands on my hips.

His eyes fill with hunger, and in a split second, I maneuver around him, putting space between us once more, which makes him smirk.

"Don't back down," he says, a hint of amusement in his voice as he turns to face me again.

"You want to fight?" I say, my brows lifting. "Here? Right now?"

He inclines his head in acknowledgement, and I drop my arms to my sides, shaking them out.

"Okay," I say, drawing out the word, "but I'm out of practice, so no vamp speed and no glamour." I walk over to the padded mats, not having to look over my shoulder to know Atlas has followed. I tug off my T-shirt, leaving me in a sports bra and leggings.

"I remain thoroughly amused you think I need any of that to beat you," he muses, again coming closer, and pulls his shirt over his head, tossing it with mine before nodding at my bra. "Your turn."

I roll my eyes, standing my ground this time. "Fuck off. Let's just do this."

"Come at me," he prompts, a glimmer of amusement lightening his eyes.

I have the stark realization that I could all too easily become addicted to this playful side of Atlas. It doesn't come out often—he won't let it—but I find myself enjoying it way too much each time it does.

I step forward, raising my arms, closing my hands into fists, and jab out with my right arm. He ducks, moving behind me, but I spin away before he can get his arms around me from behind and smack them down before getting in a punch to his chest. He advances again, grabbing my wrist and spinning me around, pulling my back against his chest. I immediately try to pull away, to escape his grasp, but he holds firm without a single ounce of effort. *Fucking vampire strength.*

"What now?" he murmurs, his lips against my ear.

My throat is dry, but I manage to force out, "Ideally, I would reach for my dagger and stab the shit out of you."

"Hmm," he says, "and where is your dagger, Calla?"

I grit my teeth, trying again to break free despite how pointless it is. There is no world where I can overpower Atlas, and he fucking knows it. "Well, I didn't think it would be very wise to wear it around a hotel with a bunch of humans."

He exhales a slow breath. "What did I tell you?"

"Not to take it off," I say in an agitated tone. "But—"

"But nothing." He snakes an arm around my waist, his lips teasing the pulse at my throat, making my breath hitch.

I flush hotly. "Fine." Then I mumble much lower, "Sorry."

"Don't apologize to me. You're the one who's dead." He bites the side of my neck without breaking the skin, as if he's intending to prove his point.

I scowl, attempting to elbow him in the ribs. "Uh, touché. Or, I don't know. Does that count if you're born a vampire? Like, you're born dead or...?"

His low chuckle in my ear makes me shiver, and I fight the urge to close my eyes and grind my ass against the very obvious erection he's pressing into me. "You pose an interesting question that I actually don't have the answer to," he says.

"Well, fuck, alert the media," I remark dryly. "That's a first."

"Cute," he throws back, nipping my earlobe. "Are you going to try to get out of this or are you enjoying it too much?"

I clear my throat. "Feels like you're the one who's enjoying it too much."

He pulls back and spins me around to face him, moving so fast the room blurs for a second. He snags my chin, forcing my gaze to his, and dips his face so his lips nearly touch mine. "You forget I can smell your arousal."

My gaze lowers as heat fills my cheeks. "Good for you."

His lips brush mine. "It's rather distracting, actually."

I lean in before I can stop myself. "Then do something about it."

His lips curve into a wicked smirk. "Perhaps once you've worked for it."

I roll my eyes, but follow him across the room to the bench press and set up the weights.

Atlas spots me while I lift. I manage a few sets before a sheen of sweat covers my chest and forehead, and I grunt with exertion, returning the bar to the rack after my fifth set. I haven't lifted that much in a while, but I feel good, *strong*. Atlas walks around the bench as I sit up, and my breath catches when he crouches at the end of it, his hands going to my hips and spreading my legs open.

"What are you…?" His hand brushes my core through my leggings, cutting my voice off. He reaches up, sliding his fingers into the waistband of my leggings, and pulls them down. I lift my ass, and he pulls them and my panties down to my ankles, leaving me bare to him. He doesn't hesitate. His tongue is between my legs in an instant, and I press my lips together, suppressing a moan.

"You know," I say breathlessly, "I really hope they don't have a security camera in here."

Atlas pauses, looking up at me from between my thighs. "I don't give a fuck."

"Noted," I breathe, and he returns his mouth to my pussy, licking then sucking my clit into his mouth. He has my head spinning in record time, and I grip the sides of the padded bench, my chest heaving with short breaths as I race toward release. His grip on my hips tightens, and he pushes his tongue deep inside me, his fingers finding the bundle of nerves at my core and driving me over the edge.

"Fuck," I moan. "Right there."

Atlas chuckles, sending vibrations straight through my core, and flicks his tongue along my pussy walls at a speed and pressure that renders me completely speechless as pleasure floods my entire body. I cry out, clamping my thighs around his head, sweat rolling down my temples as I ride the electric aftershocks of my orgasm.

Without warning, he pulls me off the bench onto the mats, hovering over me as he cages me in between his arms. "Is this enough of a distraction for you?" he taunts.

"Uh-huh," I answer, still trying to catch my breath. "You?"

"It will be."

He stands and tugs off his pants, tossing them behind him before crawling over me again, lining the head of his cock up with my entrance. My body trembles in anticipation, and I reach for him, but he grabs my hands, trapping them above my head as he slams into me, stealing my breath, and seals his lips over mine, kissing me hard and filling me to the hilt. I moan against his lips as he pulls out and thrusts back into me.

I suck in a breath when I realize his fangs have extended, and the thought of him sinking his fangs into me steals my breath anew.

"Tell me what you want," he says against my lips.

"You know."

"Of course I do," he says smugly. "I want to hear you say the words."

"You are so bossy," I grumble.

"And yet, you're so fucking wet for me because you like it and you *hate* that you like it."

"Fuck you," I growl, and he chuckles against my lips.

"What is it you think we're doing, Calla?" His blazing silver eyes flick between mine. "Now, say the words, or I'm going to stop everything."

He wouldn't. I pull back enough to glare at him.

"You think I'm not serious?"

I swallow my pride, my eyes dropping to his mouth where his fangs are visible. "Bite me." The words leach from my lips as my pulse skyrockets, and his lips curl into a dark smirk. Atlas grips my jaw, tilting my head to the side, and lowers his lips to my neck. He drops featherlight kisses there, continuing his thrusting, then a moment later, his fangs sink into my throat, and I gasp sharply. The spike of pain is quickly replaced by the most euphoric sensation that makes me sigh, and the sensation of blood being pulled from me as he fills me with his cock makes my heart pound and my head spin. A pleasure I've only experienced since meeting the vampires.

Atlas fucks me until nothing exists in my mind but him. My muscles clench around him, and I come hard, crying out as Atlas pulls away from my neck and kisses me again. His thrusts become harder and faster, until he finds his release, grunting against my lips.

We find our clothes and get dressed, and I down half a water bottle as we walk back to the suite where Lex and Kade have seemingly just gotten back.

Lex takes one look at us and grumbles, "I always miss out on the fun."

❧ 9 ☙

LEX

After what few belongings we have are packed, we check out and leave the hotel, getting into the Escalade to head for the place Marcel rented for us until we decide if we're returning to Monroe, to Washington, or where we're going next.

It's nothing fancy or like what we lived in at home, but it'll do for the time we're here. Our temporary accommodation is a simple, three-story row house with old wood floors and exposed brick walls in several rooms, including the main floor living room. There's even a small weight room on the second floor for Calla and Atlas to go at each other and a kitchen big enough for Gabriel to cook, with updated stainless steel appliances.

He and Atlas left shortly after we arrived to meet with Atlas's parents. After they found out their son was in New York City, Lenora and Simon wanted to know why. Translation: they demanded an audience with him, and Gabriel tagged along as backup. Doesn't hurt that the Yorks have a soft spot for Gabe. The guy knows how to charm anyone— old, important-as-fuck vampires or otherwise.

The plan is to tell them our trip here has to do with Selene. Gabriel's friends, Fallon and Jase, live in the city and are helping us track her down. We don't want them to know the reason we came was actually because Calla's mom was hurt and she needed to see her. They would see the move as stupid and weak, playing into the hands of the hunter who caused the accident for likely the very purpose of getting us here. Our trip has been uneventful on the hunter front so far, but our security team is very good at what they do. It would take significant manpower to get anywhere near us. After the attack at the house and the one Kade lost his sister in, we've reinforced our team tenfold. This isn't the first time the hunters have grown significantly in numbers in a short period of time and decided they were strong enough to over-throw and effectively wipe out the vampires. It seems it doesn't matter how many times history repeats, how many times the hunters lose, every handful of decades, they think they've discovered the answer to getting rid of us. Of course, it never works—it never will. Our species was made to outlast humanity... so the inconvenience of the hunters coming to interfere from time to time is just something we've gotten used to. But this time, perhaps it is different. With Calla now involved, the stakes are higher for us. The hunters—that prick Scott Ellis specifically—have something to leverage, and we have something to lose. And none of us are willing to let that happen.

While Atlas and Gabriel are gone and Kade is in the shower, I flip through the channels on the television until Calla plops down next to me. She tucks her legs under her and leans against the back of the couch, shifting her eyes toward me. "Will you tell me about the night you made the deal with my ancestor?" she asks. "Why did you do it, knowing it would ruin my chance at a future that I chose? I mean, I know you didn't know me then, but did you not think about what this would do to the person the oath was connected to?"

Well, fuck. I suppose I shouldn't be surprised that she's asking. If anything, I should be surprised it took until now. I don't have an answer. Well, not a good answer, one that will appease her. The truth is going to be sorely disappointing. I rake my hands through my hair, then drag them down my face, sighing deeply. "Calla," I say in a soft tone, "I wish I could tell you there was some important reason I needed to make that deal, but honestly, I was bored." I glance at her, and her eyes narrow ever so slightly as she shakes her head.

"You were *bored*," she echoes, disbelief filling her tone, making it sharper.

"Hey, I told you that you weren't going to be happy. That's who I was back then. I wasn't thinking about you. I figured it would be a form of entertainment when the time came. And you know, I wasn't wrong."

She scowls, and I almost wish I could take back what I said. Almost. "I'm so glad I can be a form of entertainment for you, because that's all I could ever hope for in my life. Entertainment for a group of arguably psychotic vampires who seem to hate everyone else but are okay with sharing me."

"Right," I tell her, not really knowing what else to say at that point. She's not wrong. The four of us would kill anyone who laid a finger on our girl, but we're all more than okay with each other bringing her levels of pleasure she's never and could never experience apart from us. I suppose that's what knowing one another for over a century allows for. Honestly, I haven't given it much thought. The four of us with Calla feels natural. Sometimes, it's the only thing that seems to make any sense.

"I don't understand how this bond between us works. You said it was something to do with my blood and being connected to everybody in my family line, but this feels different." Her voice softens a bit. "I mean, doesn't it?"

I nod in agreement, because she's right. It *is* different, but it has nothing to do with the oath or our connection to her blood. It's *her*, and I'm not exactly sure how to say that. "I don't know what you want me to tell you, Calla."

She huffs out a breath, and something tells me she isn't sure either. Not truly. "Tell me why you came when you did. What was it about that night? That moment in my life that you decided, *yeah, now seems like a great time to waltz in and flip everything upside down for this girl who's just trying to get through college*. Can you explain that to me, Lex?"

I pull back, surveying her face—her firm expression and the darkness in her eyes. "I know you're upset, that you've been upset since it happened—even when you didn't hate being with us. But does it really matter now? If the oath is invalid or never should have applied to you and you're free to go, does it really matter?"

"I suppose that'll be something I need to decide once I talk to Tessa. At this point, I can only hope she has some answers that you guys obviously don't."

"That's fair," I offer, kicking my legs up on the coffee table and resting my hands behind my head, my fingers laced together. "I know what I did was shitty, okay? And your reaction, knowing that it hurt you, makes me want to apologize. But then, I think that if I hadn't done it, I… I wouldn't know you. So, I can't sit here and truthfully tell you that I'm sorry, because I'm not."

She stares at me for a moment, then swallows hard. "Well." She pauses. "Thanks for your honesty, I guess."

I sit up straight and angle my body toward her. "Calla." I wait for her to look at me before I say, "You being here has changed everything. You understand that, don't you?"

I don't miss the way her pulse kicks up or the flush in her

cheeks as she stares back at me. "You know," she says in a quieter voice than I was expecting, "the time I spent waiting for you to come for me, not knowing when it would be... That was worse than anything I've faced since the night you all showed up at my apartment."

"We should have called first," I say jokingly.

She punches me in the arm, and the strength behind it makes me grin. Our girl is strong—in many ways. "You didn't answer my question," she finally says.

I nod. "You got very close to Brighton, and while we considered the possibility of that coming in handy, we were also wary of it backfiring. We decided it wasn't worth the risk and that we needed to step in before things could potentially get out of hand."

She turns on the couch, resting her back against the armrest and facing me. "What, were you concerned her dad would recruit me to the hunters and *I'd* end up coming after *you?*" She laughs as if she's kidding in her suggestion, but the thought had crossed our minds. "Seriously?" she asks, slightly taken aback.

I shrug, unsure what to make of her response. "It was a possibility we had to consider."

Calla purses her lips in thought. "And yet, Atlas insists on me carrying a weapon that can kill you and is constantly training me to—"

"Protect yourself," I interject. "He knows as well as the rest of us that you won't hurt us. Same as you know we won't hurt you." There might've been a period of time when that wasn't true, but it has certainly passed.

She huffs out a breath, pulling at a loose thread at the hem of her shirt. "Why is this so complicated?"

I itch to reach for her, to pull her into my lap and hold her against me. "Because we live in a world full of nightmares most people could never imagine."

"The nightmares have to end sometime," she murmurs.

With a sigh, I say, "Not when you live forever."

She lets out a little laugh. "You're like the worst vampire salesman ever, Lex."

My lips twitch. "Sorry, didn't realize I was in a pitch session."

She lifts her head to smile at me, her eyes holding mine. "Are… are you glad Atlas turned you? Now, I mean? Looking back on it?"

"I am," I answer sincerely. "Sure, it's had its challenges. There's no shortage of them when you have to learn a new way of living." I tilt my head, searching her face for some hint as to why she's asking.

She chews her bottom lip, nodding. "Right. Of course."

"Why do you ask?" I ask in a gentle tone.

Calla shrugs. "Just curious. You all have such different stories, it's interesting to see how you all came together."

While I don't exactly buy the entirety of her response, I don't push it. Something tells me she's not ready to explore the real reason for her question.

❧ 10 ❧

CALLA

If waking up on my twenty-fourth birthday, in an unfamiliar house, with four vampires that are, like, ten times my age isn't weird, then maybe I've spent too much time with them.

After my conversation with Lex yesterday and turning another year older today, I can't stop thinking about my future. I hadn't planned to ask him about becoming a vampire, because despite him not regretting his choice, that's still not a life I can see for myself. Immortality is, quite frankly, terrifying to consider. Add vampire hunters into the mix, and it's enough to thrust me into a tailspin of panic, so I shut down that train of thought immediately.

I make no move to get out of bed despite the warm, bright sun shining through the third story window. I lay on the soft covers, staring outside, watching people as they walk past. I'm tempted to go back to sleep; I don't think I've had a restful night in weeks. But the scent of coffee is like a siren's call, pulling me out of the comfort of the bed. I walk down the hallway and both sets of stairs, following the scent to the kitchen on the main floor. The closer I get, the sweeter the smell becomes. I step into the room and find Gabriel pulling dishes down from an upper cupboard.

He smiles the moment I enter the room. "Happy birthday, angel," he says, walking over to me with a cup of coffee in his hand. He leans in, pressing his lips to my cheek in a soft kiss, and when he pulls back, he hands me the coffee.

"Thank you," I tell him with a smile.

His eyes search mine. "Did you sleep okay?"

"Sure," I say noncommittally, and he gives me a knowing look. I shrug, taking a sip of the godly bean juice. I bump my shoulder against his. "The coffee helps."

He watches me a moment longer before letting it go, walking back to the stainless steel stove.

"What are you making?" I ask, leaning against the island in the center of the kitchen. "It smells amazing."

Gabriel keeps his back to me, grabbing a spatula off the counter next to him. "Well, I wasn't sure if you would want waffles or pancakes or French toast, so I—"

"You made all of them, didn't you?"

He turns to face me again and nods. I can't help but grin at the faint pink tinting his cheeks. *Gabriel's blushing.*

"That was very kind of you," I tell him, taking another drink. "And this is amazing. You never disappoint."

"At least where cooking is concerned," he says, then immediately looks as if he regrets saying that.

"Yeah, let's not talk about the other stuff today. Please. Can that be my one birthday wish?"

"You could have anything and that's what you want for your birthday?" Kade says, walking into the room and stealing a piece of French toast off the platter beside the stove. He doesn't bother putting it on a plate, he just folds it in half and shoves it in his mouth, eating the slice in two bites.

I press my lips together, the warmth in my chest traveling

slightly lower at the hungry look in Kade's eyes. "Well, I guess that depends," I say, "on what else is being offered."

"Whatever you want," Gabriel says, "it's yours."

I laugh, setting my mug on the island counter next to me. "I don't know if you can offer me that."

"Is that a challenge?" he asks, a glint in his eyes that shoots heat straight to my core, because I am *so* not used to this side of Gabriel, but I definitely like it.

"No," I say, "I just… I want to eat my breakfast and maybe pretend like our world isn't about to explode. Sound good?"

Gabriel nods solemnly, and Kade sighs as if he's disappointed by my request, walking around the kitchen to pour himself a cup of coffee.

By the time Gabriel finishes putting all the food out, Lex and Atlas join us in the small dining room off the kitchen. There's a floor to ceiling window at the head of the mahogany dining table which has light reflecting off the crystals from the modern chandelier hung over it.

Lex pulls me against his side and kisses my cheek. "Happy birthday," he murmurs, his lips tracing the shell of my ear.

"Thanks," I say back, wrapping my arm around him in a sort of half hug.

"So, Atlas," Lex says dramatically, "what did you get our girl for her birthday?"

I roll my eyes at Lex. "Yeah, I'm sure—Never mind. I… I don't need anything. I just want to make sure everybody I care about is safe. Which frankly seems to be too much to ask right now, so I'm good. I don't need anything."

"I was going to offer a morning training session where I might just let you win," Atlas says with a small twist of his lips.

"Yeah, I don't believe that for a second, but I'll take it. You're on."

"You know, I thought you might say that."

"That's great. Now if you don't mind, I need to eat some food. And everything smells so fucking good, I might not actually be able to move after."

"Now that sounds like the type of breakfast I'd be in for," Lex says, shooting me a wink.

"Lex, could you cool it on the sexual innuendos?"

He snorts. "As if. And you like it, don't even lie."

Instead of answering, I take a sip of coffee and shift my attention to filling my plate with a pancake, a waffle, and a slice of French toast before piling it high with syrup, raspberries, and powdered sugar. I take a seat at the table, and the guys sit around me.

"There's got to be something we can do today," Lex says around a mouthful of French toast.

I immediately shake my head. "Really, I don't want to do anything. I've never been one to care too much for birthdays, so it's all good. And we have far more important things to worry about right now than me turning another year older."

"Yeah, what are you now, thirty-seven?"

I shoot Lex a dry look. "I don't think that's really insulting until you *are* thirty-seven. And you're calling *me* old? Really?"

Gabriel chuckles from behind his coffee cup, and I turn my attention to the plate in front of me, then proceed to stuff my face.

My phone rings as I'm finishing my last mouthful, and when I see my mom's caller ID, I get up from the table and answer the call in the kitchen. "Mom, how are you doing?" I ask, finding the need to do something with my hands, so I start putting the leftover food in the fridge.

"Hang on, hang on," she says, laughing softly, and then proceeds to start singing happy birthday.

I'm surprised at the tears in my eyes by the time she finishes the song. I swallow past the lump in my throat. "Thanks, Mom," I say in a thick voice, closing the fridge as I hold the phone to my ear with my shoulder. "Seriously, how are you doing?"

"Much better."

Grabbing the sponge from the little dish beside the sink, I wipe down the island counter. "You promise you're not just saying that to make me feel better on my birthday?"

She laughs. "Calla, I'm serious. I'm okay. You don't need to worry about me. They're taking very good care of me. And so is your father, around the clock."

"Well, good, but you'll let me know if you need anything, right?" I toss the sponge into the sink and lean against the counter.

"Of course, sweetheart. Are you doing anything for your birthday?

"Um…" My voice trails off, and I chew my thumbnail. "Yeah, I think I'm going to rope one of the guys into giving me a cooking lesson. Maybe eat some cake. I hear that's customary for birthdays. But I don't want to keep you. Please make sure you're resting and not pushing yourself too hard and—"

"Calla," she cuts in. "Don't worry about me, okay? I will keep checking in with you. You will know if anything changes. I love you. Now, please go enjoy your birthday."

With a heavy sigh, I finally concede. "I'll talk to you later, okay?"

"Of course. I love you, sweetheart."

"I love you too, Mom."

"Wait, wait, wait!" Dad shouts in the background.

"Hey, Dad," I say, assuming Mom has me on speakerphone.

"Happy birthday, sweetheart," he says.

I smile, though he can't see it through the phone. "Thank you."

"You're getting old. What are you, late thirties now?"

I roll my eyes, knowing Lex is most likely in the other room laughing his ass off after having made that same quip. "Yeah, it feels like that some days," I tell him.

"Well, just know that we love you. Talk to you soon."

"Okay, Dad. I love you too."

"Bye, sweetheart," Mom says, and we end the call.

Later that afternoon, after a training session with Atlas where he does *not* let me win and in fact kicks my ass several times, Gabriel brings me into the kitchen, where he has one of the counters covered with those reusable mesh grocery bags, and they're full of food.

I turn to him, a bright smile on my lips. "You're finally going to give me a cooking lesson," I say. He must've heard me on the phone with my parents. Though I wouldn't put it past him to have already had this planned.

He nods, smiling back at me. "Better late than never."

I scan the bags, my interest piqued. "What are we making?" I ask, walking toward the counter. I peek inside one of the bags and find a loaf of French bread. I'm already excited. "I hope this is to make garlic bread," I tell him.

"Of course," he answers, coming behind me. "I figured we'd start with something fairly easy and something I know you'll enjoy because I've made it before."

"Yeah, I'm pretty sure I've enjoyed every single thing you've made, so that doesn't really narrow it down, Gabriel."

He's still smiling when he says, "What do you think about lasagna?"

"I think I want to eat it. So yeah, let's do it. What do we do first?" I ask.

"Wash your hands and then we'll preheat the oven and

start mixing the ingredients and cooking the meat and lasagna noodles."

I pull my hair back with the elastic around my wrist, sweeping it off my neck and into a messy bun on the top of my head before washing my hands, with Gabriel using the sink next to me.

He proceeds to pull out a frying pan before turning to me. "We're going to cook the meat first. I picked up ground beef. We're also going to need to cut up onion and garlic to cook with it." He sets me up with a cutting board and a knife, and I start chopping the onion while he minces the garlic.

"There's a joke in here somewhere," I tell him, glancing over at his cutting board.

He chuckles, softly leaning over to press a kiss against the side of my head. "Garlic is one of my favorite ingredients to cook with."

"That makes me so happy," I tell him. "I could live off garlic bread. You know, if it was sustainable." Once the onion and garlic is chopped, we add it to the frying pan with the ground beef, and I mix it all together over the burner, then lean against the counter while it cooks. "What's next?" I ask him.

"We'll add the tomato paste and sauce as well as crushed tomatoes with some water and seasonings once the meat is cooked."

"That seems simple enough," I tell him, pursing my lips.

"Yes, this recipe is not as complex as it is lengthy. You do have to simmer it for a while. At least an hour, I've found, while stirring it occasionally to prevent it from sticking to the pan and burning."

"Wow. You should have your own cooking show." My tone is teasing, my lips twisting up at the corners.

"You think so?" he asks with a grin, and I nod in response. He cages me in, his arms gripping the counter on either side of me, and presses his forehead against mine. "I know you said you're not one to celebrate birthdays, but I for one am very grateful for your birth."

My cheeks flush, and I close my eyes as his lips brush mine. I lean into him, sealing my lips over his and kissing him deeply. His hands drop to my hips and pull me against him as his tongue slips into my mouth and he kisses me as if I'm the first breath of air he's taken in days.

My world narrows as my head spins and warmth floods my chest—and much lower when I feel the hardness between his legs press against me.

"You know, I had a feeling Gabriel would be a hands-on teacher in the kitchen." Kade's voice reaches me, and Gabriel chuckles against my lips, pulling back and kissing my cheek before stepping away. Kade walks around us to the fridge and pulls out a blood bag, ripping it open and drinking directly from it without even warming it up or putting it in a glass. He slides onto the counter beside where we were working, drinking in silence with his eyes locked on me.

I pull my bottom lip between my teeth to keep from frowning at him. Instead of responding to his behavior, I busy myself pulling out the necessary ingredients to make chocolate cupcakes to go with dinner. I mix the batter while Gabriel continues working on the lasagna, sticking my finger in the bowl and sucking the sweet, chocolatey goodness off before pouring it into a cupcake pan. My eyes whip toward Kade at the sound of his low growl and my cheeks flush as his eyes devour me.

"Do you need to take a walk?" Gabriel asks him.

His lips twist into a smirk. "That's not what I need."

I prop my hands on my hips, staring at him pointedly. "You want to help me make the icing?"

He slides off the counter and comes towards me, tossing the empty blood bag on the counter behind me. "Hmm, that depends," he says in a low voice, dragging his tongue over his bottom lip. "Do I get to lay you across this counter and lick it off you?"

A laugh escapes me before I can stop it, though neither of us miss the jump in my pulse. "It's my birthday. Maybe I should get to eat off you."

His smirk widens. "You will hear no arguments from me on that." He moves at a speed I can't track, grabbing my hips and lifting me onto the counter. His mouth is on mine before I can take a breath, and I make a startled noise against his lips. Without thinking, I wrap my legs around him, pulling him as close as he can get with the counter there, and he kisses me hard. My heart slams against my ribcage when I feel his fangs extend, but he's careful not to let them slice into my lips.

When he pulls back to give me a chance to catch my breath, his eyes flick between mine, and my gaze drops to the bulge in his pants before swinging toward Gabriel, who is watching us with hunger in his eyes.

"You want in on this, Gabe?" Kade says in a smooth voice.

I don't wait for him to answer. I reach out, offering him my hand. He steps closer, taking it and letting me pull him toward Kade and me. Once he's close enough, I slide my fingers into his hair and bring his mouth to mine, kissing him as warmth flares to life in my stomach.

Kade slides his hand up my thigh slowly, teasing me while one of Gabriel's hands finds its way under my shirt, the other braced on the counter. His mouth explores mine, his tongue pushing past my lips and flicking across the roof of my mouth. I push my chest into his touch, and he cups my breast, making me thankful I didn't bother with a bra after my post-training shower. His fingers circle my nipple before pinching it, making me gasp against his lips at the same moment Kade spreads my legs open, pressing his thumb against the heat at my core through my leggings.

"I want to bury my cock here," he says in a husky voice that sends shivers through me, because fuck, I want that too. "Hmm," he hums. "But first, I want a taste of our birthday girl."

Gabriel pulls away from my lips, sliding his hand to my hip, then uses both hands to lift me just enough for Kade to peel my leggings and panties down to my ankles before tugging them off completely.

My bare ass is on the counter we were just preparing food on, and that feels all kinds of wrong—for about five seconds.

My focus narrows on Kade's head between my legs. He trails his lips from my knees up the inside of each of my thighs until I'm practically squirming. Gabriel guides me backward until I'm laying across the island countertop. He pushes his hands under my shirt, dragging it up until my breasts are exposed, then pulls it off over my head. He leans over the counter and kisses me slowly, deeply, his fingers brushing over my collar bones, featherlight, until they reach my chest. I tip my chin up to kiss him back, moaning into his mouth as he cups my breasts, massaging them with skilled fingers as Kade continues to torture me with his teasing kisses against the delicate skin of my inner thigh.

"I've barely touched you, and you're already dripping for me," Kade purrs, and my cheeks flush hotly. He's right; moisture seeps from me, my core throbbing in response to his words.

His tongue flicks out, licking up my slit, and I practically whimper against Gabriel's lips. My back arches off the counter, pushing my breasts into his hands.

Kade sucks my clit into his mouth, swirling his tongue

around it, and plunges two fingers into my pussy, making me see stars.

I cry out, breaking my kiss with Gabriel, my chest heaving with short breaths. "Fuck," I breathe, my hips moving against Kade, pushing him deeper inside me.

He thrusts hard and fast, curling his fingers at just the right angle to have me moaning in seconds. Heat shoots straight to my core and I clench around his fingers, riding them as his mouth devours me, licking and sucking at alternating speeds and pressures until my head is spinning. Gabriel continues palming my breasts, rolling my nipples between his fingers. His lips find the sensitive skin of my neck just below my ear, his breath stirring the hair there. "Are you going to come for him, angel?" His words propel me closer to the edge, the muscles in my stomach coiling tight.

"Yes," I pant. "Kiss me."

His lips are on mine in a second, devouring me as thoroughly as Kade is. My heart pounds in my chest and my head feels light enough to float away. I'm floating on a cloud of blissful pleasure that I would give anything to last forever.

Seconds later, my pussy clenches around Kade's fingers and I'm launched over the edge, overcome with an earth-shattering orgasm that has me moaning against Gabriel's lips and grinding against Kade's face and fingers as I ride it out. He licks me clean before straightening and helping me sit up as Gabriel comes around the counter, leaning next to me.

"One down, twenty-three to go," Kade comments with a smirk, licking his lips.

I stare at him, still trying to catch my breath. "What the hell are you talking about?"

Gabriel shakes his head, chuckling softly. Clearly, he understood what Kade meant.

"Birthday fucks," Kade says.

I choke on a laugh, taking the shirt Gabriel offers me and

tugging it on. "Do you want me to live to see my twenty-fifth birthday? Because I'm pretty sure letting you fuck me twenty-four times in one day would kill me."

᠅

After eating far too much lasagna and garlic bread at dinner, to the point my jeans are too uncomfortable to stay in, I slip away to the bedroom to change into leggings.

There's a soft knock at the door as I'm tying my hair back.

"Come in," I call out.

A moment later, Lex slips into the room, closing the door behind him. "Are you ready to go?" he asks, his gaze sweeping over my clothes.

I arch a brow at him, shaking my head. "Go where, Lex?"

The corners of his mouth curl into a grin, and I'm immediately suspicious. "Do you trust me?" he asks.

I prop my hands on my hips. "I don't know how to answer that."

He walks over to me at an easy pace, and part of me wants to step back, but I stand firm, though my hands drop to my sides as those silver eyes search mine. "Do you trust me?" he asks again. His tone is devoid of any humor, so I take a moment to consider it. I press my lips together, unable to form a response. Lex grins. "You didn't immediately say no, so I think we're making progress."

I roll my eyes. "Yeah, okay, so what? Where are we going?"

"I think it's time you get a tattoo," he says.

I blink at him. "Just because I didn't say that I don't trust you doesn't mean I'm going to let you tattoo me, Lex."

He reaches for me and tweaks my chin before I can move or slap his hand away. "We'll just see. How about this? I'll let you tattoo me if you let me tattoo you."

I lean against the dresser, staring at him. "You realize I have no experience in repeatedly stabbing somebody with a needle, right?"

He shrugs, as if that's the least of his concerns. "You'll catch on quick."

"Okay," I say, drawing the word out. There's a mix of nerves and excitement in my belly, making me antsy. The weight of his gaze doesn't help either. "Are you serious?" I check.

His only response is a confident grin.

There are several beats of silence before I sigh heavily. "Let's do this."

He offers me his hand, and I find myself reaching for him without even thinking about it. Our fingers lace together, and we walk downstairs to the main floor, where the others are lounging in the living room.

"I can't believe you convinced her," Kade says, sipping his glass of whiskey. I'm not sure if he's drinking more blood or booze these days, but it seems to help. To numb the anger and sadness radiating from him since he lost his sister for the second time. As much as it hurts me to see, if that's how he needs to cope right now, who am I—or any of us—to interfere? Kade doesn't seem like the type who would respond well to an intervention, though I do still think we need to do *something*. The anger and guilt and sadness he's harboring would rip even the strongest person apart.

"Honestly, same," I tell him. "This is crazy, right? Like, I shouldn't do this."

Kade shrugs. "It's not the end of the world, Calla. It's just a tattoo."

"Yeah, just a permanent marking on my body. Not like it's forever." My tone is dripping with sarcasm, but I press my lips together at the last word. *Forever*. Heat gathers my cheeks, and I drop my gaze to the floor. Something about the word holds new weight, and I have a feeling it has to do with the people I'm sharing my life with. Perhaps it's another reminder of my mortality. Knowing that Lex, Kade, Gabriel, and Atlas will live forever, whereas my life is a ticking clock.

"Come on," Lex says, tugging on my arm, and we head outside where the Escalade is parked at the curb. Lex opens the passenger side door for me to climb in, then shuts it and moves around the front of the vehicle using vampiric speed. In the time it takes me to blink, he's behind the wheel, starting the engine.

"Let me guess," I say as he shifts the car into drive and pulls onto the street. "You know another tattoo artist?"

"Not exactly," he says in response, pressing the gas harder.

I turn and look at him, my brows drawing together. "Uh, what does that mean?"

"Well," he says, drumming his fingers against the steering wheel. "Let's just say I found a tattoo studio that we're going to *borrow* tonight."

My eyes widen, and I smack his arm. "Lex! We're going to break in somewhere?"

He grins without looking at me. "You don't need to sound so horrified. I'll leave money."

"Yeah, and what if we get caught?" My voice increases in pitch with each sentence.

"Then I'll deal with it," he says, amusement lacing his tone. "You need to chill."

I shake my head, staring out the windshield. It shouldn't surprise me that Lex planned to have us break into a tattoo studio in the middle of the night. And the more I think about it, the less it does surprise me. What actually does is the lack of reluctance on my part. I trust that Lex will take care of it if something goes down. If the cops show up and try to bust us, he'll glamour them to fuck off. So really, the stakes aren't that high. At least in that respect. I'm absolutely still panicking over the thought of letting him near me with a tattoo gun. And yet, here I am. I don't think he would have forced me into the vehicle back at the house if I'd flat out refused, and I'm not sure if that says more about my progress with him or vice versa.

I exhale slowly, stretching my legs out and say, "All right."

"See?" he says, "This is gonna be great." He cranks up the music, filling the space with The Weeknd's *The Hills*. The bass makes the car vibrate, and I close my eyes, getting lost in the music. Lex rolls down the windows, letting in the crisp late-April evening air, and I breathe deeply, allowing myself to enjoy this moment, however fleeting and temporary it may be.

The tattoo shop is in one of the nicer neighborhoods in the area, and as we get closer, I can feel the nerves radiating off Calla in waves. She has to know I'm not going to let anything bad happen, otherwise she wouldn't have gotten into the car. If she didn't want to be here, she wouldn't be.

I park the car on the street and hop out, walking around the front and opening Calla's door, offering her my hand.

She stares at me, her expression filled with uncertainty and her lip caught between her teeth.

"Come on," I encourage with a charming smile, leaning toward her. "We do have all night, but I have other things planned for you I'd very much like to get to."

Her eyes narrow slightly, though the slight tinge of pink in her cheeks makes me think her head went the same place mine did. Finally, she takes my hand and allows me to help her out of the Escalade.

"We can't exactly walk through the front door," she says. "I'm sure they have a security system."

I shrug. "I'm sure they do, which is why we're gonna go through the entrance at the back and also why I had Marcel's team hack into their system and disable any alarms."

"This is quite the elaborate birthday gift, Lex. Breaking and entering. Wow, so nice of you."

I laugh softly, squeezing her hand as we walk to the back of the tall and narrow, gray brick building through an alley between it and what smells like a butcher shop, and come to a stop at a solid metal door. I purse my lips, looking at the lock. I could probably try picking it but it'd be easier just to break it, so that's exactly what I do.

Within seconds, the door is open, and I usher Calla inside, closing it behind us. I keep the main lights off as we walk down a short hallway, our shoes echoing off the black marble floor. The space smells of citrus-scented cleaning products and antiseptic. There's also a bit of cologne that lingers in the air. I had scoped out the place earlier while Calla was training with Atlas and knew it would work perfectly.

I peek into one of the rooms and find it set up with a padded chair and a tattoo station, so I guide Calla inside, flicking on the light. The floor in here is white, contrasted by black walls with a gold zig-zag pattern. There's a shelf on the wall across from the door that's lined with black binders— samples of the artist's work, no doubt, considering there isn't any on the walls like in most places.

"You're going to show me how to do this, right?" she asks, pulling her hand free from mine and holding it up to look at it. Her fingers are shaking a little, and she presses her lips together. "I'm not sure this is such a good idea. I'm not going to be able to stop shaking the entire time, and your tattoo is going to look like a toddler did it."

I can't help but grin at that. "You're cute."

"Yeah, you're not going to think that when I fuck up the

art that is currently on your body."

"Whatever you do is going to be perfect," I tell her, "but if it makes you feel better, I can glamour away your nerves, steady your hand."

She steps back immediately, her posture stiffening and her breath hitching. "You know I don't like it when you guys do that."

I hold my hands up in a gesture that's meant to be calming. I don't want to ruin this evening before the fun has even started. "I know. I'm not saying we have to, I'm saying it's an option. Whatever you want."

After several beats of silence, she huffs out a breath and plops down on the rolling stool. "Okay, I... Fine, I guess. But it better be temporary and very specific to what we're doing. And please make whatever it is you're having me draw on your body very simple and small and—"

"You're overthinking this," I cut in using a light tone, walking over to her. I slide my finger under her chin, tilting her face up so her eyes meet mine. "This is supposed to be fun. Relax. I'm not worried and you don't need to be either. Just have fun and enjoy your birthday."

"I don't think my idea is the same as yours when it comes to fun."

"Hmm, I think we both know that's not entirely true," I point out, smirking.

"Fine," she concedes and rolls toward the tattoo station, looking over all the instruments, and picks up the tattoo gun. "What am I supposed to do with this? Just draw?"

I cough to cover the sound of my laugh and shake my head subtly. "There's a little bit more to it than that."

She sets the gun down and shoots me a dry look before pulling her hair back. "Well, you're going to have to show me."

I nod. "Okay. What do you want on you?"

She seems to consider that for a moment, her eyes trailing the length of my bare arm to the vines and roses there.

"I don't think you're ready for a sleeve just yet," I tease.

"Funny," she deadpans. "I don't know. What do you think I should get?"

I shrug. "It's your body. It needs to be something that represents you or something you love. Or it can be fucking random, it doesn't matter. You can put as much or as little thought into it as you want. People get tattoos for all kinds of reasons, some for no reason at all. What do you think about the outline of an orchid? Maybe somewhere along your wrist or your thigh? I mean, you can put it somewhere you can cover up if you want or somewhere you can see at all times. It's totally up to you."

She tilts her head back and forth, thinking about it, then says, "Yeah, I like that idea. Something minimal and delicate. Maybe on the side of my wrist going up towards my elbow?"

I nod. "We can do that no problem."

"Okay, so what are you entrusting me to put on you?" she asks.

"I figured I'd let you do whatever you want."

She bursts out laughing. "That is very dangerous. I am no artist. I need a very simple design with an easy to follow stencil, and also maybe a shot of something strong to convince me this isn't the worst idea in the world."

"Fair enough," I say, more than a little amused with her. "I'm sure I can find something around here. And that might help steady your hand. Do you want to go first?"

"Uh, I guess?" she says, though it sounds more like a question with the increase of pitch near the end. "How long is it going to take?

"Ten, maybe fifteen minutes tops. The design I'm thinking for you is quite simple, not a ton of detail or shading necessary, so it won't take long at all. It'll take longer to set every-thing up than it will to actually tattoo you."

"Okay." She drags the word out, nodding as if she's talking herself into it.

I pat the chair and say, "You get settled in here. I'm gonna go find something to drink and be right back." I pause in the doorway, feeling the need to make sure she's on board and comfortable with being here. "You can still change your mind. If you truly don't want to do this, we don't have to." The corner of my mouth tugs up. "Believe me, I have no problem jumping to the second part of our plans for tonight." My cock twitches in my pants just thinking about taking her in that chair.

Calla folds her hands in her lap, looking at me with a bright-eyed expression. "No, I want to. Ever since that night you took me to Scarlett's, I've thought about getting one."

"Okay. Sit tight, birthday girl." I shoot her a wink, and she switches from the stool to the lounge style tattoo chair as I leave the room to search for a bottle of liquor. It's not diffi-cult to track down. In fact, they have essentially an entire bar set up in their kitchen. I snag a bottle of tequila and head back to the studio, where Calla is lounging on the chair, her legs crossed at the ankles, staring up at the ceiling as her fingers tap along her thighs.

I saunter back into the room, the bottle of tequila in my hand, and walk around the lounge chair to drop onto the stool. I crack the bottle open, taking a long swig before handing it to Calla for her to do the same.

She swallows a mouthful, cringing, and sucks in a breath after she swallows. "That tastes like shit," she says.

I chuckle. "Yeah, well, it's an acquired taste. Are you ready?" I ask.

She puffs out her cheeks and offers a nervous laugh. "Yes?"

"Is that a question?"

"No. I mean, yes, I'm ready. Let's do it." She holds the bottle of tequila in her lap while I turn and start preparing the ink and gun after pulling on a pair of black gloves. "Aren't you gonna make a stencil?" she asks. "I mean, I don't have a lot of experience when it comes to tattoos but from what I've seen, they usually do."

I glance at her over my shoulder. "If that will make you more comfortable I can, but it's not a difficult design. I was planning on free-handing it."

She hesitates, pursing her lips. "Don't fuck it up," she says, offering me a hard stare.

I nod, barely containing my amused grin. "I thought you trusted me to do this."

"I do. I just don't want a wonky orchid on my arm."

"All right, I'm going to do a stencil, because you're just going to—"

"No, Lex, it's fine. Just do it."

I shoot her a wink, then turn back and continue preparing the instruments. When the gun is loaded up, I turn back to her and shave the small portion of skin I'm going to be inking. "Ready?" I check.

Her eyes meet mine, and she nods. "On a scale of, like, one to ten, how bad is this going to hurt?"

The corner of my mouth tugs upward. "It'll hurt far less than me sinking my teeth into you. How's that?"

Her cheeks flush and she looks away. "Yep. Okay, cool."

"No need to get uncomfortable, Calla." Especially considering how much we both know she likes to be bitten. I don't bother saying it aloud—I don't need to. My cock hardens just thinking about it.

"I'm not," she insists. "Just start before I freak out for no reason and change my mind."

"Okay," I say, lowering the gun to her skin. I start the

design that I had pulled up on my phone, going for a few seconds before stopping. "How's that?" I check.

"Huh," she says, surprise filling her tone. "Yeah, that's not bad actually."

I can't help the smugness in my voice when I say, "I told you."

She rolls her eyes. "Yeah. Okay, just keep going."

The entire design takes about ten minutes. When it's done, I set the gun down and rip off the gloves, tossing them into the wastebasket on the other side of the table. I wipe her skin clean and let her take a look at the design. "You like it?"

"Holy shit. I'm kind of obsessed."

"That's good, considering it's kind of permanent."

She grins, still looking at the tattoo.

I wrap it up and tape the bandage to make sure it heals properly.

"Can I tell you something?"

I don't miss a beat. "Anything."

"I really don't want to tattoo you."

I laugh deeply, sliding my hands up her thighs. "It's okay. I wasn't going to make you do it."

"I'm not saying I couldn't do it," she points out. "I'm just saying I really don't want to fuck it up."

"It's all good," I tell her. "It's your birthday. We can do whatever you want."

She presses her lips together, her eyes flicking between mine. "The entire time you were sticking a needle in my skin, all I could think of was—"

"That time at Scarlett's?" I cut in, tilting my head to the side.

She nods, placing her hands over mine, her thumb tracing back and forth across the top of my hand. "I mean, we're already here. We've already broken probably multiple laws by breaking in, so we might as well—"

Before she can finish her sentence, I tug her forward, slamming my mouth against hers, claiming her lips with my own.

❧ 12 ❧

CALLA

My world narrows on the feel of Lex's mouth on mine. He braces himself on the back of the chair with one hand as he leans over me and slides his other hand into my hair, gripping the back of my neck and holding me in place.

Our lips move together, battling for control in a way that makes my pulse surge and my heart pound against my chest as if it's attempting to break free of my ribcage.

I grip the front of his shirt, wanting him closer, pressed against me everywhere possible. I push my tongue into his mouth and grin against his lips when he groans in response.

After a blissful moment, Lex pulls back a little. "Tell me what you want," he murmurs, his lips brushing the line of my jaw.

I keep my eyes closed, licking my lips. "Whatever you're thinking," I say, slightly breathless, "that's what I want." Lex has never been one to disappoint, and right now, I really don't want to have to think.

He drags his mouth down my throat, kissing softly and making my skin tingle at his touch. "You'll need to be wearing far less clothing for what I'm thinking," he says in a low voice, looking at me with a dark, hungry gaze, though his fangs aren't visible—yet.

I nod, reaching for the waistband of my leggings to tug them down. Lex grabs my wrists and in a nanosecond has them above my head. I gasp softly, not expecting the movement.

"Keep them here," he instructs. "Let me take care of you."

I bite my lip, gripping the headrest of the chair and nodding.

Lex's eyes glimmer with amusement as they trail the length of me, from where my nipples are sticking out against my T-shirt to my Docs. He slides his hands up my thighs, warming the skin beneath my leggings, and I hold my breath as he gets dangerously close to the heat between my legs. His hands reach my hips and he drops them inward, brushing his thumb over my clit, making me gasp. His eyes flick to mine, darkening with desire. "You know," he murmurs in a husky tone, "I was going to reward you for handling your first tattoo so well, but I think I'll make you work for it a little longer."

My eyes narrow. "Mean," I grumble.

He presses his thumb down, and my hips lift at the same moment a moan tears its way from my lips. "Needy little thing," he muses.

"If you don't touch me," I say, holding his gaze, "I'll touch myself. You're more than welcome to watch."

Lex shakes his head, tutting his tongue. "Hmm, no you won't. I told you to keep your hands where they are."

I arch a brow at him. "You also said it was my birthday and we could do whatever I wanted. I didn't think you'd torment me before fucking me."

"Patience," he says in an amused tone, leaning in and

brushing his lips across mine in a whisper of a kiss before pulling back again.

I scowl, though the sound is half-hearted. "You may have forever, but I certainly don't."

Lex chuckles and finally curls his fingers into the waistband of my leggings, dragging them slowly down my legs until they fall onto the floor in a pile along with my panties. "I'm dying to bury my cock in that sweet pussy of yours, so this is torment for me too."

"So shut up and put us both out of our misery."

He smirks. "Oh, I will, but first I think I'll make you come with my tongue. I want to taste you just as badly as I want to fuck you."

Heat fills my cheeks and pools low in my stomach. My skin feels ultra heightened, and when Lex presses his mouth just below my belly button, I pull my bottom lip between my teeth, my core throbbing with need.

The first pass of his tongue along my slit has me trembling, closing my eyes and fighting the urge to grip his hair and grind against his face. He holds me open to him, swirling his tongue around my clit until I'm panting, and when he plunges it inside me, I clench around him, unable to stifle my moan. Lex sucks and licks and thrusts his tongue in and out, pulsing his fingers against my clit in perfect timing. In minutes, I'm panting, desperate to feed the need to come. My breasts tingle, and I want nothing more than to reach for them, but I'm concerned Lex will stop fucking me with his tongue if I disobey his instruction to keep my arms above my head.

He hits a particularly sensitive spot deep in my pussy, and I suck in a sharp breath, moaning his name. He picks up speed, devouring me with his mouth as I writhe against him, my fingernails biting into the back of the chair. Pleasure floods through me in waves, and I succumb to it, crying out my release as a powerful orgasm rips through me. Lex licks me clean, making me shiver as I continue to ride the delicious aftershocks. He kisses the inside of each of my thighs before pulling back, grinning at me. He holds out his hands, and I take that as permission to move my arms, taking his hands and letting him help me sit up. I'm still catching my breath when he drops a soft kiss against my temple and murmurs, "I'm going to fuck you now." In what feels like less than a second, Lex unbuttons his pants, pulling his cock free and stroking it a few times.

Before he can make a move, I lean forward and lick the blunt head, making him hiss out a sharp breath.

"Calla—"

"You had yours, now I get mine," I say before swirling my tongue around him, pushing him into my mouth until he hits the back of my throat.

Lex closes his eyes, gripping the counter behind him. "Fuck. You are perfect. So fucking perfect."

His words make my heart beat faster, and I bob up and down his cock, taking as much of him into my mouth as I can, and reach out to massage his balls in my hand. I want to drive him crazy like he does to me. And based on the way he's biting his lip and thrusting his hips forward, I'm heading toward that accomplishment pretty damn quickly.

"If you don't slow down, I'm going to—"

I pick up the pace, using my other hand to pump the base of his cock as I swirl my tongue along the rest of him. He curses, grabbing the back of my hair but continuing to let me control this. A few more thrusts, and his balls tighten in my hand as he grunts and spurts his release onto my tongue. I swallow it down and pull back, wiping the back of my hand across my lips before grinning up at him.

He pulls me off the chair completely, lifting me up, and I

wrap my legs around his waist, holding onto his shoulders as he grips my hips.

"I'm nowhere near done with you, but this maybe isn't the best place for the rest of what I have planned."

My eyes widen, a flush creeping across my cheeks. "Oh?"

He leans in, pressing his forehead against mine. "Two words."

I laugh, giving him a chaste kiss. "We are not playing strip poker."

Lex groans, letting me down. "Way to be a party pooper, birthday girl."

After we put our pants back on, we head out to the car. I'm surprisingly giddy over it for having been so nervous at the thought of giving Lex control like that, but I'm thrilled with the outcome. The tattoo is a delicate outline of an orchid and it's easy enough to cover up—not that I can see myself ever wanting to.

There's a warm tingling between my thighs which is more pronounced than the itch of my new tattoo. Having my way with Lex in the tattoo studio made me think of the night at Scarlett's place in Washington where I had sex with him for the first time. His intensity knows no bounds and steals my breath every time. I've come to crave it like an illicit drug, and I ride the high of what we did the entire way to the house.

He helps me out of the Escalade, lacing his fingers through mine, and we walk inside together.

Kade is lounging on the couch in the living room with a half empty wine glass of liquid too dark and thick to be wine, and Atlas is sitting across from him with his nose in a book. He glances up when we enter the room, his eyes landing on the bandage around my wrist and his lips twitching briefly. "Do I want to know what he convinced you to get?"

"What, you don't want to see my *Calla loves Atlas* tattoo?

The heart around our names is the best part." My voice is dripping with fake sweetness, but the sarcasm laced through it sort of negates it.

He arches a brow at me, looking as if he's going to respond but instead lowers his gaze back to the book in his hand.

Kade sits up, peering over the back of the couch at us. "Seriously," he says, "what did you get?"

I can't help but smile thinking about the gorgeously simple design. "An orchid."

"An orchid?" he echoes. "What the fuck is an orchid?"

Lex snorts, giving my hand a gentle squeeze. "It's a flower, you dumbass."

"Her favorite," Gabriel says, walking into the room from behind us. He pauses at my side, leaning in and kissing my cheek before going to the chair opposite Atlas.

"And it's stunning." I squeeze his hand this time. "Lex is an artist, in case you guys didn't know." I stifle a yawn, slipping my hand free from his. "Now, if you don't mind, I'm going to get changed. I'm about ready to pass out, but you four feel free to play strip poker without me."

"Where's the fun in that?" Lex asks, frowning at me.

"Not fucking happening," Atlas chimes in.

I laugh softly, walking out of the living room and upstairs to the room I've been staying in.

My phone chimes with a new text as I'm getting changed. I grab it off the nightstand to find a message from an unknown number wishing me a happy birthday. My stomach clenches, and I can't help but hope it's Brighton. Instead of responding to the text, I call the number immediately. The line rings and rings, and just when I think it's going to click over to voicemail, the call is answered. There's dead air for several seconds before I say, "Brighton? Brighton, is that you?"

"Happy birthday, Calla."

My eyes fill with tears, my throat clogged with emotion. I press my fist against my lips to hold in the sound of my tears. "Thank you. I... I don't know what to say. I'm so sorry about what happened to your mom. She didn't deserve that. *You* didn't deserve that. I wish there was something I could do to make it better. I want to be with you, to be there for you. I can't even imagine what you're going through right now. I... I almost lost my mom and I can't—I just... I'm so sorry, Brighton."

"You want to do something?" she asks. There's an edge to her voice that makes me tense. "Because there is something that you can do to help me."

I catch my bottom lip between my teeth, hesitating before I ask, "What is it, Brighton?"

"I know you're in New York City. I know what happened to your mom, and I'm sorry, but if you want to help, you can trick those vampire friends of yours—those *monsters*—and lure them to the hunters. I can text you a location. They'll take care of them for good, and you can have your life back. You never wanted this, did you? I can help you get free of them."

My stomach drops at the coldness of Brighton's tone, and her words make me want to vomit. "I... Brighton, I can't." Those are the only words I can muster. My head is spinning. Just the thought of betraying the guys makes me want to cry. Despite how they came to be in my life, I'm in a place now where I can't imagine it without them. And even if I could—even if I decided to walk away from them—I would never be okay with turning them over to be executed.

The silence on the line is deafening and seems to last forever. Until she says quietly, "Then you're not really sorry, are you?"

My mouth drops open, my chin quivering as my vision blurs with an onslaught of hot tears. "That's not fair."

She sighs, sounding more agitated than I've ever heard her before. "Look, I know you think you care for them, and maybe they've even done some nice things since they kidnapped you weeks ago, but it's not real, Calla. You never had a choice in any of this."

I squeeze my eyes shut, silent tears rolling down my cheeks. "You're wrong," I force out, my voice breaking near the end. "I may not have chosen to be with them in the beginning, but whatever I feel *is* my choice. Brighton—"

The line goes dead, leaving me distraught. Bri is just in shock. She's trying to figure out how to grieve the loss of her mom, and in her own mind, she probably thinks she's trying to protect me. But this isn't really what she wants. She didn't mean it when she asked me to send the guys to their deaths. If she believed I truly cared for them, she wouldn't ask me to do something that would cause me so much pain I can't put it into words. Because, yeah, if something happened to one of the guys, that would fucking hurt.

My hand shakes as I open the text conversation and type out, *I'm so sorry. I love you.* I wait for a few minutes, dropping onto the end of the bed and staring at the screen. But when no response comes after ten minutes, I set my phone beside me and fall back against the mattress, tears leaking out the corners of my eyes as I stare at the ceiling.

At that moment, I make the very conscious—albeit potentially stupid—decision not to tell the guys about what Brighton said. If they were listening, they heard it anyway, but I'm not going to bring it up if they don't.

As much as I don't want them in danger, I'm worried if they know what Brighton asked me to do, they'll decide she needs to be dealt with along with her dad, and that terrifies me.

LEX

Calla's bestie wants us dead.

I suppose that's fair, considering her mother was killed by vampires, but that doesn't excuse Brighton asking Calla to help lure us out for the hunters to attempt to pick off.

Will she come out and tell us or will she decide to keep it from us?

The call ended abruptly almost an hour ago, and Calla hasn't come out of the bedroom since. Fifteen more minutes pass before she comes out, and I approach her in the hallway.

"I was wondering if you were going to join us again," I say, grinning softly. "How's the arm?"

"Huh?" She shakes her head, refocusing on me. "Oh, it's fine. Kind of itchy but it doesn't hurt."

I nod. "That's normal." My eyes dance across her face, looking for any hint she might give up the information I'm waiting to hear.

"Yeah," she says absently. "Um, thanks again. Maybe you can show me another time, and I'll try it on you."

I nod slowly. "Is there anything else?"

Her pulse jumps and her eyes narrow a fraction. "What do you mean?" she asks, swallowing hard.

I shrug. "Nothing in particular. I was just curious. You look like there's something on your mind."

"Lots," she says.

"Anything worth noting?" I press.

"Is there something *you* want to talk about, Lex?"

I shake my head. "I don't know, Calla, is there?"

"Okay, why are you being weird?" She crosses her arms over her chest, pinning me with a glare. "And since when do you beat around the bush?"

I step closer, right into her personal space. "I thought I would give you a chance to tell me yourself."

Calla stands her ground, her expression as tense as her posture is rigid. "I don't know what it is you want me to tell you."

"Hmm, I'm pretty sure you do." I snare her gaze, putting glamour behind my words as I say, "Tell me about the phone call with Brighton."

She visibly shudders, gritting her teeth and staring at me hard. A few seconds pass. It turns into a minute, and she doesn't speak but she does look downright pissed, her eyes flashing with anger and her hands balling into fists at her sides.

"That is so fucking annoying," I grumble, preparing to try again.

Gabriel comes up the stairs before I have a chance and says, "What's going on?"

I focus on Calla, lifting a brow at her. "Do you want to tell him, or should I?" I offer.

She looks as if she's about to tear my head off, which if I wasn't so pissed, would be an absolute turn on. She keeps her arms crossed and focuses her attention on Gabriel, speaking to him as if I'm not even here. "Brighton texted me from a new number, so I called her. I think she's in a really bad place since her mom was killed and I think Scott got to her because—"

"She wants to kill us, essentially," I cut in, leaning against the wall in the hallway. "And she wants our girl to help."

Calla blows out an agitated breath. "It's not *you* in particular, it's just… it's vampires. Vampires killed her mom. She doesn't know—"

"You're just coming up with excuses for her because you don't want to admit your bestie is a vampire hunter now."

She glowers at me. "We don't know that she is. Wanting vampires dead and being the one to kill them are two different things."

"What did she say to you, angel?" Gabriel asks in a level, calm tone. Always the fucking voice of reason, Gabe is.

"Well, she… she wanted me to get you guys somewhere the hunters could take you out." She shrugs. "I don't know where. She said she'd send me a location, but that was before I told her I couldn't do what she was asking."

Gabriel frowns and nods. "I see. Was there anything else?"

Calla shakes her head. "I tried to talk to her, but she hung up on me. She knows about what happened to my mom and that we're here. I just—I'm worried about her."

"Oh, that's sweet," I remark in a dry tone. "You're not worried about us?" It's petty, but the thought of anyone threatening my brothers puts me on high alert, and this situation has me agitated as hell.

Calla's brows tug together and her gaze flips between Gabriel and me. "Of course I'm worried about you, but we have each other. Who does Brighton have besides her psychotic father, who, for all we know, is manipulating Brighton to do his dirty work?" Her tone is biting by the time she finishes her sentence. She's come to loathe Scott Ellis as much as the rest of us after he almost killed her mother, and

I suppose we should consider the possibility that sick bastard would use his own daughter to get what he wanted—the four of us dead.

"What, you're her only friend?" I say anyway, still pissed Calla was going to keep this information from us.

"I'm her only friend that knows about vampires. I just… This wouldn't have happened if you guys had let her come with us."

"I understand you're upset, angel. We'll talk more about this tomorrow, but for now, try to get some rest." He shifts his attention to me. "I'm going to go talk to Atlas," he says, touching Calla's arm in what I think is meant to be a comforting gesture, before walking away.

Calla attempts to walk away too, but I step in front of her. She sighs. "Lex—"

"You can't keep secrets from us, Calla."

Her lips part in surprise before she scowls. "That is a two-way street if you want me to hang around." Her eyes widen as if her own words shocked her, and she pushes past me, hurrying away.

We haven't discussed the blood oath connection and what'll happen if we discover it has no bearing on Calla, but that comment—and her reaction to it—makes me think she's thought quite a bit about it.

I fight the urge to go after her. Instead I take a page from Gabriel's playbook, knowing he would suggest I give her some space. She's under an immense amount of stress, and while she seems to be mostly adjusted to having us in her life, we can't expect her to be okay with everything that goes along with that.

I can't help but feel a little bad for upsetting her, but any information about the hunters is incredibly important. Knowing that does nothing to diminish the pit in my stomach, and I make a mental note to speak to Calla later on and apologize for trying to force the information out of her—not that it worked. I think at this point, the rest of us are just as intrigued and curious about how she's able to resist our glamour as she is.

That witchy friend of Gabriel's sire better have some fucking answers.

❧ 14 ❧

CALLA

The next morning, I wake with my stomach in a ball of nerves. My head is spinning, trying to come up with all the questions I want to ask Tessa about the blood oath and my newfound ability to occasionally resist a vampire's glamour. None of it makes sense, and part of me is worried that even if she's able to answer my questions, I still won't have the clarity I'm so desperately searching for.

I take a shower to try to wake up and calm my nerves, scrubbing my skin with a rose scented body wash and standing under the hot spray of water far longer than necessary to wash my hair. I eventually force myself to get out, dry off, and put on a pair of black high-waisted jeans, tucking in a white tank top. I comb my hair and apply a little bit of makeup to make myself look a bit more alive before heading downstairs to the kitchen to get a cup of coffee.

Gabriel is standing next to the coffee machine, sipping from his own mug, and smiles when I walk into the kitchen. "Morning, angel," he says softly.

"Morning," I say back and approach as he pours me a cup. "Thanks," I murmur, taking it from him.

"Are you ready for today?" he asks.

"Yes and no," I answer honestly. "I think I'm putting too much hope in getting answers from Tessa, and surely that's not fair to her."

Gabriel nods in understanding. "Tessa has been a part of this world for quite some time. If anybody can help, it's her."

I take a sip of my coffee, nodding. "Thanks again for setting this up."

"Of course," he says. "We'll head out in a few minutes. When you're ready, okay?"

"Sure," I say.

Atlas walks into the room with damp hair and a black V-neck that is at least a size too small for him and clinging to the hard muscles in his stomach. My eyes get stuck on his arms, and I lift my mug to cover the flush of my cheeks

His eyes shift between Gabriel and me, holding mine for a moment. "I've ensured we'll be the only ones in the café, and Marcel has a team that will sit outside and secure the building."

With a sigh, I say, "This is ridiculous." While the security team is quite good at discretion, the thought of constantly being monitored is creepy. You'd think after looking over my shoulder everywhere I went in the years leading up to the guys coming for me I'd be used to feeling as if I was being watched all the time. I thought that would stop since I joined the ones who were watching me. How wrong I was.

"It's for your safety," Gabriel says in a gentle tone. "And for ours as well. We can't be sure what the hunters are planning, and considering Scott knows we're in New York City, we can't be too careful."

"I understand," I say, setting the mug on the counter. "Are you coming with us?" I ask Atlas.

"Yes. We're all going."

"Super," I remark dryly. I'm sure Tessa is going to be

thrilled with my posse of testosterone. I'm not fully versed on the history between the vampires and witches, but I do know they aren't BFFs. I'm lucky she agreed to this meeting, otherwise I really have no idea where I'd go searching for answers.

Atlas doesn't crack a smile. Instead, he turns and walks out of the room.

"Geez," I mutter, "who shit in his cornflakes this morning?"

Gabriel offers a faint smile. "He's just concerned for everyone, that's all. He takes a lot of responsibility in keeping the people he cares about safe. Which, believe it or not, Calla, includes you."

I press my lips together, unsure how to respond to that. The thought of Atlas giving a shit about anybody, especially me, is hard to swallow. But the more I think about it, something deep inside me knows it's true—and that same part knows I care just as much for him.

❧

The café is completely empty of patrons when we arrive except for one round table near the back of the room where Tessa sits, watching the door as we walk in, the old-fashioned bell above our heads chiming to announce our entrance. Her bright emerald eyes flash with recognition when they land on me, and she stands, offering a wide, unreserved smile as we approach that somehow eases a good amount of the nerves in my stomach. I realize as I walk across the worn hardwood floor that, despite the circumstances of this visit, I'm happy to see her. A hell of a lot more than the last time when Selene sent her.

"Hello again," she says, tucking her ink black hair behind her ear to reveal a line of dainty silver studs along her earlobe. Today she's rocking a plum-colored blouse tucked into acid-washed jean shorts and shiny black Doc Martens that I'm immediately obsessed with. I'd much rather be meeting up to go shopping with this girl than to discuss supernatural shit, but here we are.

"Hey," I say, jerking my thumb behind me. "Sorry for the entourage."

She presses her mauve-stained lips together against a smile and nods. "It's okay. I understand. Do you want to sit? I assume your guys bought this place out, so we might as well get something to drink and eat. I'm starving."

I laugh softly, surprised at how genuine it sounds. "Yeah, that sounds good."

Tessa and I sit across from each other at the small table while the guys pile into one of the booths along the front window not far away, chatting softly. We both order chai tea lattes and chocolate croissants. Tessa also orders a yogurt parfait and a fruit salad. She munches on the fruit as she says, "So, what can I help you with?"

I take a deep breath, glancing sideways toward the guys before I focus my gaze on her. "I'm not sure how much you know about why we're together. Essentially, my family made a deal with them—Lex specifically—wherein the firstborn daughter from my bloodline would be promised to them for saving the life of my ancestor who got into some shady business a long time ago. Fast forward to when I was born, they thought the oath was being fulfilled with me, but my mom had given birth to a baby girl prior to me. The baby died shortly after she was born, but she did live for a period of time. Basically, we need to know if that child fulfilled the oath, meaning it doesn't—or never really did—apply to me."

Tessa pauses, her fork halfway to her mouth, then sets it down, leaning back in her chair. "That is… Wow, I'm sorry. That's a lot."

"Yeah," I say with a breathy laugh. "I only recently found out about it, so the last time we met, we didn't know about this."

"Right," she says, tapping the side of her mug with a black-painted nail. "I suppose..." She pauses, pursing her lips in thought. "Magic is tricky, but that sounds like a loophole if I ever heard one. That baby girl your mom lost is who would've 'belonged' to your vampire friends over there. You are the second born Montgomery daughter, correct?"

"Yes," I say in a quiet voice, my stomach clenching painfully.

"Well, I think that's your answer, Calla."

I frown, my heart pounding in my chest. Though I'm not sure if it's because Tessa just told me that technically I'm free, or because now I have to decide whether or not I'm going to stay with the guys.

"Not the answer you were hoping for?" she asks, flicking a glance towards the guys.

I shake my head. "I just... I wasn't sure what to expect."

"Care to elaborate?" she offers.

"For the better part of two months, I thought we were connected because of the oath. Because of some mystical connection between our blood, but—"

Something like understanding flashes in her eyes, cutting me off.

"What?" I ask warily.

Tessa smiles at me, her expression thoughtful. "Calla, whatever connection you feel to them has nothing to do with magic."

My stomach drops at the certainty in her tone, because as scary as it is, deep down, I know she's right. "Right, well..." I trail off and clear my throat. "We're sort of dealing with a lot of different things right now and this is just an added level of complication." That reminds me of Tessa's connection to

Selene, and I take a sip of my latte before I say, "No offense, but you seem too nice to be friends with someone like Selene. I mean, have you met her?" Not the subtlest shift of topic, but I'm desperate to veer away from the whole feelings conversation, especially with the guys well within earshot.

Tessa pops a blueberry into her mouth, offering a short laugh. "We're less friends and more acquaintances through debt." Her gaze drops to the table for a few seconds before she meets my eyes again. "Selene saved my life a long time ago, which left me indebted to her. That's the reason I agreed to spell your blood against the vampires. I owed her one and I didn't have a choice."

"She saved your life? Selene? We're talking about the same vampire, right?" Sure, she stopped Dante from draining me like a juice box, but only to torment and hold me captive herself. "Can I ask what happened?"

"Yeah, I mean, it's taken me some time to move past it, but it was back when I discovered what I was. I obviously didn't know what magic was prior to that night. When I was born, my parents put me up for adoption. They suppressed my magic with a cloaking spell in hopes of giving me a normal life. But when I got old enough, the spell failed and my magic went out of control. I didn't know how to handle it—I didn't even know it existed." She pauses. "I accidentally set fire to my adoptive family's home."

I keep my mouth shut so my jaw doesn't drop open, but my eyes still widen. "What happened? I mean, did they…?"

"They survived," she says, nodding. "Barely. The authorities couldn't figure out how the fire started and how I was unharmed, so they decided to send me to a psychiatric hospital. Somehow Selene caught wind of what happened and she knew—or she could guess—it had something to do with magic. She intervened and took me somewhere I could learn to control and use my magic. So, yeah, I kind of owed her."

"Wow, that's intense."

"You can say that again. It hasn't been easy. Learning everything and living in this world—the witches, vampires, hunters—but I think it's important you decide what you really want. And even if it's not the easiest option, you have to fight for it. You and I are the same in that we have a time-line, Calla. We are mortal and our time on this earth is limited. If we don't do what is right for us, I think that's the biggest tragedy of all."

I'm surprised at the tears gathering in my eyes and I blink them away quickly, nodding at her. "There's something else," I say. "I have, on occasion, been able to resist the vampires' glamour. I have to really focus, and if I'm vulnerable in any way emotionally or otherwise, like if I'm tired, it doesn't work. Do you know anything about humans resisting glamour?"

She tilts her head to the side, regarding me curiously. "No," she says, her tone laced with surprise. "I mean, *I've* learned to mostly resist it, but there are still some vampires, depending on their age and their pedigree, that are still able to get past my defenses, but I have magic at my disposal. I'm kind of baffled that you're able to."

I rake my fingers through my hair, sighing. "Cool. So I'm a supernatural anomaly. That's great."

She chuckles softly, and I hear one of the guys snicker behind us. My money's on Lex. "I'd like to see it, if that's okay?"

My stomach clenches at the thought of willingly having the vampires try to glamour me, but I reluctantly agree with a single nod.

We all get up and walk to a more open area of the café, pushing some tables out of the way. Gabriel steps up first, and Tessa stands at the sidelines, watching closely as Gabriel meets my gaze and murmurs in a hypnotic tone, "Lift your right leg."

The muscles in my leg tense, and I clench my jaw, unable to break his gaze. I imagine putting all of my weight into my leg to keep my foot planted on the ground, visualizing that it's glued there by cement and there's no chance I have the strength to lift it. A few seconds pass. Then a minute. Finally, Gabriel blinks, severing the glamour, and my muscles relax.

"Interesting," Tessa muses.

Gabriel offers me a smile, and I turn my attention to Tessa. "Yeah, but it doesn't work all the time."

"No," she agrees. "It's definitely mind over matter. I could see you fighting it with the way your body tensed and the crease between your brows. You really had to put some thought behind how you were resisting it."

"Right," I say, "but sometimes I can't get to a place where that's possible."

"I understand what you're saying. I'm not sure there's a workaround for that. I could stand here and tell you not to get emotional and you'd be able to resist glamour whenever you want, but the reality of that is it's not always possible."

"How is it *ever* possible?"

"Hmm, I can't say with complete certainty, but it likely has to do with your emotional connection to each other."

Shifting the weight between my feet, I say, "If that's true, I probably can't resist glamour from a vampire I don't know or have a connection to."

"That's right. Sorry, I know it isn't convenient. The fact you're able to resist *any* glamour is impressive."

"Gee, thanks," I remark dryly.

She offers me a knowing smile. "Do you want to try again?"

I shrug, blowing out a breath. "Sure, why not?"

Tessa glances between the vampires, then points at Kade,

who shakes his head. "I'm good. I'll just observe." His voice is detached, his eyes unfocused.

I frown, worry creeping in again, but Tessa doesn't seem to notice as she skips past him and moves to Lex, who shoots me a wink as he walks closer and captures my gaze. "You want to punch Atlas in the face." His glamour washes over me, and I ball my hands into fists at my sides, fighting to put up a mental block against his words.

I shake my head. "You don't need to glamour me for that to be true," I remark dryly, and he bursts into laughter, Gabriel and Tessa chuckling as well.

"That's cute," Atlas says in a dry tone, taking Lex's place in front of me. His glamour slams into me without warning, and I immediately know I'm in trouble. "Take your dagger and stab Lex in the shoulder."

My hand is reaching for the weapon before I can even attempt to stop myself, pulling it from the holder at my thigh. I spin around to face Lex, moving at a speed I didn't even know I was capable of. He's able to stop my arm, gripping my wrist so tight I drop the dagger before I can stab him with it. The pain lancing down my arm severs the glamour, and I blink hard, shaking my head to clear the fog there. Lex frees my wrist, and I bend to pick up the dagger, returning it to the holder before turning back to Atlas and Tessa.

"Two out of three isn't bad," she says. "Plus, Atlas here is stronger than the others based on his bloodline, so you did quite well."

Atlas shoots me a smug grin, and I flip him off.

Tessa and I return to the table for her to grab her things.

"Thanks again for meeting me. I really appreciate it."

"Of course," she says, lowering her voice. "And listen, I know what I told you might not have been what you wanted to hear, but the choice is yours to make. I can't offer you advice. If you knew more of my history, you probably wouldn't want it anyway. But feel free to contact me whenever."

I pull her into a hug, I think surprising both of us, and smile at her when I pull back. "You too. Don't be a stranger. Oh, and nice shoes."

Tessa glances down, her lips curling into a grin. "I have to confess, I bought them after meeting you and seeing yours. They looked so cool, and I've never owned a pair. I rarely wear anything else now."

My smile widens; I can't help it. "I hope you know, we just became best friends."

"Hey, no arguments here. I think we could both do a lot worse," she jokes.

We laugh, walking toward the front door, and Tessa offers a quick wave to the guys on her way past. Pausing in the doorway, she turns back to me and says, "Keep me posted on things, yeah?"

I nod, sliding my hands into the pockets of my pants. "Definitely."

"Take care, Calla. I'm sure we'll chat soon."

"You too," I tell her, then watch her get into the back of a town car. As the car pulls away from the curb and drives away, I frown at the pang of sadness in my chest. I've never had many friends, and connecting with Tessa so easily is making me miss Brighton.

Instead of returning to where Lex, Atlas, and Gabriel are sitting, I find Kade at the counter, munching on what looks like a carrot muffin. "I want to talk to you."

"Lucky me," he says, swallowing, and sets the muffin on the counter. "To what do I owe the pleasure?"

"Kade," I say softly, shaking my head. "I... I'm worried about you. We all are. You've been off for a while." I press my lips together. I can practically feel the darkness in him, and it scares me. Even more, thinking he's going through this alone makes it ten times worse.

"You don't need to worry about me, Calla. I don't want to add to the weight on your shoulders."

I grab his face, holding on even as he tries to pull away. "Kade, I promise you, we will make the hunters pay for the pain they've caused, for the damage they've inflicted. I will learn how to fight and I will kill them myself."

His eyes soften a fraction and his hands go to my hips, pulling me closer. "I've done nothing good to deserve you," he says in a voice barely above a whisper, dropping his forehead to mine.

I close my eyes and press a kiss against his cheek. "It's gonna be okay," I murmur before pulling back. I take his hand, and we walk over to the others, where Gabriel is drinking what looks like a cappuccino and Lex is stuffing his face with a croissant.

Lex wipes his mouth and stands, taking my other hand. "My turn." Kade lets go of my hand, and Lex pulls me aside.

"What is it, Lex?" I'm really not in the mood for another lecture from him, and honestly, after everything today already, I don't want to talk anymore.

He stares at the ground for a few seconds before lifting his gaze to meet mine. "I'm sorry for yesterday. It was wrong of me to try to force information from you, no matter what it was in regards to. I'm sorry for upsetting you."

I blink at him in surprise. The last thing I was expecting was for Lex to apologize for, well, anything. I nod slowly. "Thank you, I appreciate that. And I do forgive you. I understand why you did what you did, but please don't do it again. That being said, I'm sorry I was going to keep information from you that could have turned dangerous. I was scared and I didn't know how all of you would react. I'm *still* scared.

Brighton is my best friend, and if anything happens to her, I don't know what I'll do."

Lex nods this time. "We'll figure it out, okay?" He holds his hands out, and I slide mine into his. He wraps his fingers around my hands and squeezes reassuringly. "We still have a lot to talk about, but I know how overwhelmed you are, so why don't we just take a beat, yeah?"

I exhale a heavy breath. "Please."

Lex lets go of my hands, slinging his arm around my shoulders as we walk back to the others. "Oh, and one more thing? Next time Atlas glamours you to stab me, could you try just a little harder to resist?"

15

LEX

I passed out on the couch last night after about six too many glasses of whiskey, evidenced by the ache in my neck when Calla shakes me awake the next morning.

"What is it?" I grumble without opening my eyes. I can already tell the sunlight streaming in through the living room window is going to burn when I do manage to pry them open.

"Lex, get up." The tone of her voice, the seriousness of it and the worry it's filled with, make my eyes fly open.

I cringe as I sit up. "What's going on?" I demand.

"Kade is gone," she says. Dark circles line her eyes, and the tension in her jaw has me standing in an instant.

Dread floods through me, heavy as concrete, settling in my gut, and my fang slices through my gums before I can even try to hold them back. "What do you mean, *gone?*" My voice is as close to desperate as it gets, and I grab her shoulders, needing an answer right fucking now.

Gabriel comes into the room with Atlas behind him. "He wasn't here when we woke up," Gabe says.

Fuck.

Fuck.

One of two things has happened. Either Kade lost his shit and took off, or the hunters have him. The former seems likelier than the latter, considering the rest of us are still here and unharmed. If the hunters came for us, they wouldn't have just taken Kade and left us alive. If anything, they would've taken Calla to get to us. That thought makes me growl, my grip on her shoulders tightening. "We should've kept a closer eye on him. We knew he was struggling—we should have made him talk or get help or… fucking *something*, I don't know." Guilt claws at me, its talons sharp and unforgiving.

Calla grabs my forearms, digging her fingers into my skin until I realize I'm probably holding her too tightly and ease my grip. "We'll go look for him," she says, her forehead creased with worry. "And *when* we find him, we will—"

"I'll go," Atlas cuts in, shrugging on his worn black leather jacket. It's nearly May, though the cold weather in New York seems to be lingering.

Calla steps away from me and grabs her jacket off the back of the couch. "I'm coming with you."

"You're not." His voice is firm, but I see the fire in her eyes.

"Atlas, now is *not* the time—"

"You're not coming with me. Stay here."

She tries to walk to the front door when Atlas turns his back on her, but Gabriel catches her around her waist pulling her back. "Are you fucking kidding me right now?" she demands. "Kade is gone. We should all be out looking for him."

Gabriel remains calm despite the cold glare Calla is shooting at him. "It's not safe. Atlas will find him," he insists in an attempt to placate her.

"If it's not safe for us, it's not safe for them," she counters, pulling away from him, though she doesn't attempt to follow after Atlas.

"Atlas knows what he's doing," I chime in, raking my fingers through my hair, which I'm sure looks extra crazy from sleeping on a couch cushion. "He will be fine. He'll find Kade and bring him back here. Everything will be fine, Calla." I'm talking to her but also to myself, repeating the words over in my head in hopes that I'll manage to trick myself into believing them. I have complete confidence in my sire; Atlas will find Kade wherever he ran off to, but I get Calla's urge to join the search. I feel it too.

She blows out a frustrated breath, the faded Pink Floyd T-shirt she slept in riding up and exposing a sliver of her stomach. "This is ridiculous," she says, shaking her head. "We can't catch a fucking break."

Gabriel's phone chimes, and he pulls it out of his pocket, reading it over before he says, "It's from Fallon. They found Selene and want to know what they should do."

Great. Another problem. What fucking impeccable timing.

"I'm going to give her a call." He glances between me and Calla. "Are you good to handle this?"

I nod in response, and Gabriel slips out of the room, leaving me alone with Calla. I walk over to her, snagging her chin and tilting her head up to look at me. "Breathe," I tell her. "I see you slipping and I understand. Everything keeps getting piled on, and if I had to bet, you probably feel help-less right now." *I sure as hell do.*

She pulls her face away from me, exhaling harshly. "Yeah, just a bit."

"I think we need a distraction. You up for a game of hide and seek?" I ask with a grin. It's more than a little forced, but I hold it anyway.

Calla laughs, giving me an odd look. She thinks I'm kidding.

"I'm completely serious," I say. "You go hide…" I lower my voice, then add, "and if I find you, I get to do whatever I want with you." I smirk at the jump in her pulse and the heat my words bring to her cheeks.

She crosses her arms over her chest as if to hide the perkiness of her nipples, though I can still sense just how excited my idea makes her. The sweet smell of her arousal makes me want to throw her onto the couch and take her right now. Fuck the game.

"Hmm, okay, I'll play. But you do have a slightly unfair advantage, supernatural senses and all, plus being able to use our connection to find me. It won't be a very fun game when it's over in five seconds."

I hold my hands up. "I promise, no vampire abilities. Until I find you, then they're fair game." I'm dying to sink my teeth into her again. Not to mention, I'd give anything to bury my cock between her thighs, because I need the distraction just as much as she does.

She chews her bottom lip, considering it. "Okay, fine. But if you cheat—"

"I'm not going to cheat, Calla. Now, you have ten minutes." I meet her gaze and offer a dazzling, albeit slightly predatory smile. "Time to hide."

Her eyes widen before she takes off out of the room and down the hall. I listen for a few seconds before purposely pulling back my heightened senses, staying true to my word.

I poke my head into the kitchen, where Gabriel is still on the phone with Fallon. He nods at me, letting me know he'll fill me in later, and then I proceed to start searching the rooms on the main floor before heading upstairs.

Either Calla is really fucking good at this game, or I am shit without my vampire senses, because thirty minutes go by, and I still haven't found her.

I'm walking out of the bedroom she's been staying in with

only a few more rooms to check when the faint creak of a hinge catches my attention down the hall. I pause, pressing my back against the wall, and wait. She must be in that bedroom waiting for a chance to change hiding places, perhaps to somewhere I've already searched. It's a smart plan in theory, but she's about to be caught. My gums throb at the thought of capturing her, and I lick my lips.

A moment later, Calla darts out of the room, spotting me a second later. She curses and makes a break for the stairs. I catch her easily, snaking my arm around her waist and pulling her against me halfway down the stairs as I chuckle victoriously.

Between one moment and the next, Calla sinks her teeth into my shoulder hard, and I let go of her, cursing in surprise. She catches the banister to keep herself from falling and rushes down the rest of the stairs—only to run right into Gabriel. He steadies her, glancing past her to me, and I offer him a grin. His eyes darken slightly as they shift back to Calla, and in a flash, he has her over his shoulder, carrying her up the stairs toward one of the bedrooms as she curses him out for not playing fair. I follow behind them, my cock hardening and my gums throbbing even more now, to the point of pain. I fight to keep my fangs retracted as I close the bedroom door behind us.

Calla isn't getting away this time. And I'd say, with the way her heart is trying to beat out of her chest, she damn well knows it.

Gabriel sets her down far gentler than I would have, and the moment her back hits the mattress, she scrambles up toward the headboard and tries to get off the bed, losing her sweatpants in the process when Gabriel grabs for her ankles and pulls them clear off. He doesn't make a move to stop her further, and she gets around him, stopping in her tracks when her eyes land on me. Her gaze flicks toward the door before returning to me.

I shrug. "Go for it."

She narrows her eyes at me as her pulse kicks up. "This doesn't feel like hide and seek."

My lips curl into a smirk. "It's not. I won that game." I take a step toward her, and she presses her lips together. "This is my prize. And Gabriel's, because I like to share. I'm a good friend like that."

Calla rolls her eyes. "Technically, Gabriel caught me. *You* lost me."

"You *bit* me," I toss back at her, very much enjoying the ping pong of banter we've got going on.

"Touché," she deadpans.

I offer her a grin and delight in the soft gasp that escapes her lips when my fangs extend.

Gabriel moves silently behind her, sliding his arm around her waist and caging her against his chest. Before she can protest, he presses his lips against her neck, and she leans into him, her head tipping back onto his shoulder as she catches her bottom lip between her teeth. Her gaze holds mine as Gabriel reaches around her with his free hand, sliding his fingers into her black lace panties. Her eyes widen a moment later, and she pulls in a shallow breath before her eyelids start to flutter shut.

I move closer, my erection protesting being trapped beneath the fabric of my pants. I reach forward and rip the little bit of fabric off of her. "Eyes on me," I order, sliding my hand into my pants and freeing my cock. I stroke myself, watching Gabriel thrust his fingers into Calla's pussy as he holds her against him, no doubt grinding against his own erection.

Tension coils tight in my stomach as I increase the speed of my hand, and Gabriel matches his thrusts in time with my pumps. Calla's eyes bounce between my face and my cock, her cheeks flushed and her expression filled with arousal. Gabriel tweaks her clit, and she moans, arching against him.

"Are you going to come on his fingers?" I ask in a husky tone, my breathing increasing as I continue pumping up and down.

She nods, biting her lip.

"Say it."

"Fuck off," she hisses, reaching back to bury her fingers in Gabriel's hair and pressing her lips against his collarbone. She breathes hard against his skin, grinding her hips into him as he adds another finger and uses his thumb to circle her clit.

Calla is panting now. "I can't… I'm going to… My legs are going to give out."

Gabriel's lips trace the shell of her ear. "It's okay, angel. Let go. I've got you."

Her moans get louder, and Gabriel once more increases the speed of his thrusts, pushing her over the edge. She cries out at the same moment her knees buckle, and Gabriel stays true to his word, catching her before she collapses. He carries her back to the bed, setting her on the end of it before tugging off his shirt and sliding in behind her. I waste no time fitting myself between her thighs as she falls back against Gabriel. He moves back so she's nearly laid flat and rubs her shoulders in a slow, circular motion, eliciting a soft moan from her. I lift her shirt, pressing my lips against her stomach, then take my cock in my hand and trace back and forth along her entrance.

Calla shivers, her chest rising and falling fast. "Lex…"

"Don't worry," I say in a soft voice, "I won't make you beg." I slam into her, stealing her breath. I bury myself in her warmth, all the way to the hilt, and groan at her tightness. I will never tire of this feeling, of Calla wrapped around my cock. "Hmm, Gabriel got you nice and wet for me." Her release makes it easy to thrust in and out at a quick pace, and I lose myself in the feeling of her pussy clenching around my cock, milking me as she moans without abandon. The sound is fucking music to my ears.

I pound into her, pressing down on her hips and groaning as pleasure fills me, shooting to my cock and tightening my muscles. I grunt, slamming into her hard and fast, and find my release just a few thrusts later, spilling my release deep inside her.

Calla's climax follows only moments later, her hands gripping the bedsheets on either side of her and her head thrown back against Gabriel's chest.

"Holy shit," she breathes, the muscles in her thighs twitching as I pull out of her.

I chuckle softly, my own breath stilted, and offer her my hands. When she takes them, I pull her into a sitting position, and she glances back at Gabriel—more specifically to the bulge in his pants. She turns and crawls up the bed to him, sealing her lips over his. I'm not sure what I want to see more —Calla riding him or swallowing his cock.

"Angel," he says softly, gripping her hips.

"You haven't come yet," she points out in a soft voice. "And you technically won the game." She kisses him again. "Take your prize."

"Are you sure you're ready for more?"

Ah, Gabriel. Always the gracious lover.

She nods. "I'm ready for *you.*"

Gabriel smiles at her as if she's his world. "Hang onto my shoulders, yeah?" He licks his lips, pulling his thick, solid cock out of his pants. "I want you to ride me."

Calla's pulse jumps as she nods again, holding onto Gabriel's shoulders and lifting herself up. I watch from the end of the bed as she lines him up with her entrance and sinks down onto his cock, letting out a low moan as she takes all of him.

"That's it," Gabriel murmurs, holding her hips steady.

She lifts up, then drops back down, making Gabriel groan, tipping his head back against the black wrought iron headboard as he watches her through hooded lashes, his eyes ablaze with lust... and something deeper than that.

Calla picks up speed, nearly bouncing on his cock less than a minute later, her breaths coming hard and fast as she pants, gripping Gabriel's shoulders so tight her fingernails have left indents in his skin.

"Yes," Gabriel says, holding her gaze and thrusting his hips up each time she slams down on him. "Don't stop, angel. You're doing so good."

"Mmm," she hums, circling her hips and moaning loudly. "I'm so close."

"Come for me," he says, pulling her against him, and captures her mouth with his. Their movements become quicker and near-frantic as they chase each other to orgasm.

She breaks the kiss, panting hard. "Gabriel... *ahh.*"

"Yes," he groans. "That's it. Come."

The sounds of their combined release fills the room, and I can't tear my eyes away. Watching them is so fucking hot. My cock is twitching, ready to take her again. Gabriel too.

Calla collapses against Gabriel's chest, his cock still buried in her pussy, and she stays there as their breathing returns to normal.

"That's it," I say, smacking the mattress. "When Kade and Atlas get back, we are *finally* playing strip poker."

Gabriel chuckles at the same moment Calla scowls, and I just grin at both of them.

16

CALLA

By the time Lex, Gabriel, and I pull ourselves out of bed and have lunch, over an hour has passed. I volunteer to clean up and wash the dishes, considering Gabriel cooked and, quite honestly, I could use time to myself with a slightly less sexually charged distraction.

I'm just about done loading the dishwasher when the front door flies open, slamming into the wall. I hurry into the hallway and suck in a sharp breath when I see Kade next to Atlas—covered in blood.

Gabriel and Lex show up behind me in an instant, then very deliberately step around and in front of me. Kade, on the other hand, doesn't look at me. He simply drops his chin and walks upstairs. A moment later, the bathroom door slams shut and the shower turns on.

The rest of us gather in the living room. I linger in the doorway while Atlas, Lex, and Gabriel sit around the coffee table.

"Where did you find him?" Lex asks, his voice deep with concern.

Atlas sighs, pushing his fingers through his hair, and I

can't help but notice how absolutely exhausted he looks. It makes my chest ache; we're all wearing thin. Atlas's eyes meet mine briefly before he turns his attention to Lex. "I found him," he says, "with his teeth stuck in a... *professional dancer* at a club about thirty minutes from here."

Gabriel frowns and Lex scoffs. "A professional dancer? He was fangs deep in a stripper?"

Atlas sits back, rubbing his jaw. "By the time I got there, he had killed half a dozen people."

"Fuck," Lex says in a low voice.

Gabriel closes his eyes a moment, shaking his head, and lets out a sigh. "It's good you found him. A spectacle like that was just asking for a hunter ambush."

I push away from the doorway, turning to walk back into the hallway. They don't need me to be part of this conversation, but there's a pressure in my chest that makes me think the vampire upstairs does.

"Where are you going?" Atlas says, and I don't turn back around.

"I'm going to check on him." Despite the ice that shot through my veins hearing what he had done, my need to comfort him outweighs any fear I might have.

"That's not a good idea," Atlas warns.

"He won't hurt me," I say over my shoulder, though it may be more to convince myself than the others. Even if something happens, there are three other vampires who would have my back.

I force my legs to carry me down the hall and up the stairs, pausing outside the bathroom, my hand hovering over the doorknob. I take a deep breath before I slip inside, closing the door behind me. The room is hazy, filled with steam and the all-glass floor to ceiling shower is fogged up, though I can still see Kade's broad form under the rainfall showerhead. His hands are braced on the white marble tile, his head bent forward as the water hits his back. Blood rolls off of him, staining the tile at his feet. He doesn't acknowledge my presence for a few seconds, and when he speaks, he doesn't look at me. "You shouldn't be in here." His voice is practically unrecognizable. It's dark, vicious, as if he hates me. It feels like a punch to the gut. I want to turn and leave— I don't want to see him this way. But I can't. My feet are rooted in place.

"I'm not leaving," I say, surprised at the steadiness of my voice. I walk closer to the shower, and he finally turns to meet my gaze, his silver eyes slamming into me like a freight train. I swallow hard at the menacing expression on his face. His fangs are protruding from his gums, and he makes no attempt to retract them. He's trying to scare me away, but I refuse to give into it, to the fear that wants me to believe that Kade is a monster who doesn't care about anything or anyone, when I know full well that isn't true.

Instead of leaving, I pull off my shirt and drop it on the floor, then step out of my shorts, leaving myself naked before him.

The darkness in his eyes—at least some of it—shifts to something I'm a little more familiar with. Hunger. Lust.

The muscles in his shoulders tense. "Calla," he warns.

I close the rest of the distance between us, opening the shower and stepping inside before I can talk myself out of it.

"What are you doing?" he demands, turning to face me as the water cascades onto my face.

"You are not alone," I say firmly, reaching for him.

He grabs my wrists in a tight grip, pushing me until my back hits the opposite wall. He lifts my arms over my head, pinning them against the wall. "Do you know what I did?" he whispers.

My stomach drops. "I… Yes."

"What makes you think I won't do the same to you?"

I force myself to hold his gaze despite the pounding in my chest and the alarm bells blaring in my head, screaming at me to get away from him. "Do you want to?" I ask in a quiet voice.

He lowers his face until his lips are at my ear. "I want to fuck you so hard I can't think straight. I fear that it's the only way I can escape the horrors playing on repeat in my head."

"You're worried that's going to scare me away?" I ask.

"No, Calla, I'm worried that I'll lose myself. That I'll lose control and tear your throat out to devour your blood."

I nod slowly. "Yeah, I'd rather you didn't do that."

He laughs harshly, the sound void of any humor.

He's hurting so badly, so deeply. There's nothing I can do to fully erase that pain, but maybe I can numb it for a short while. Offer him some bit of reprieve.

I lean forward as much as I can with my wrists trapped against the wall and press my lips to his. Kade stands frozen for a moment before he slowly starts to kiss me back. He takes a step closer, his chest touching mine, and my nipples harden as I feel the hardness between his thighs against my stomach.

"Let me touch you," I say against his lips and tug on my wrists.

He holds them against the wall, water dripping down his face as he pulls back just enough to look into my eyes. "You want to touch me? To stroke my cock until I can't hold back any longer and climax with your name on my lips, covering you with my release? Is that what you want?"

I can't read the tone of his voice—I also can't deny how hot his words are making me. Because yes, that's exactly what I want. "I want to take care of you."

His grip tightens for a moment before he releases me, his hands trailing the length of my arms, then down my stomach. He steps back, and I lower my arms, flexing my fingers a few times to get the blood flowing again. As hot as being pinned against a wall while naked is, it does get uncomfortable after a while.

Instead of wrapping my fingers around his erection, I sink to my knees in front of him. His broad upper body blocks the water from hitting me, and I lean forward, licking the head of his cock. I swirl my tongue over the tip a few times, looking up at him. His eyes are blazing, liquid silver that I immediately get lost in.

"Keep teasing me, and I'll fuck your mouth raw," he warns, his tone low and jagged.

After a few more swipes of my tongue, I close my lips around him and suck, pulling him into my mouth. A rush of excitement zips through me and heat pools low in my stomach when Kade hisses out a sharp breath before groaning.

"Hmm," I hum, making my lips vibrate against his cock. I pull back, flicking my tongue over his head before taking him back into my mouth, hollowing my cheeks as I suck on him.

He grabs the back of my head, and my pulse races, but I give myself over to the idea of bringing him pleasure in hopes of helping him through what I can only imagine is one of the darkest periods of his incredibly long life. I let him guide me up and down his cock, relaxing my jaw as he thrusts his hips forward, filling me to the back of my throat.

"Do you want me to come in your mouth?" he asks in a thick voice. "Because if not—"

I grab his ass, sucking harder in response.

"Fuck," he curses, breathing hard. His grip on my hair loosens a little, but I don't relent. I bob up and down until Kade stiffens, grunting as he climaxes and shoots his release onto my tongue and against the back of my throat.

I swallow what I can as he steps back, his cock gliding

over my tongue as he pulls it out of my mouth, then let the water wash away what spilled over my lips.

Kade helps me up and slants his mouth over mine the second I've taken a breath. Our kiss is fiery. It's a battle for control, and I'm not giving in this time. Not even when he grabs my chin, tilting my head back slightly to deepen the kiss.

"Fuck me," I breathe, tugging him closer and pressing my forehead against him. "Lose yourself in me."

"I could hurt you."

"So hurt me," I offer, my voice strong, unwavering.

His eyes widen, filling with horror, and he recoils.

"There," I say quickly. "That look on your face right now is why I know you won't."

"Calla." My name on his lips sounds desperate. I'm not sure if it's a prayer or a curse.

I drape my arms over his shoulders and press my breasts against him, licking my lips. "I'm here," I tell him, kissing each of his cheeks. "It's okay."

His gaze holds mine and his throat bobs when he swallows. "Turn around."

I bite my lip, nodding, then pull my arms back and do as he says. I'm facing the shower wall with my back to Kade, my pulse pounding beneath my skin as I wait for him to make a move.

Kade wraps his hand around the back of my neck and presses me flush against the marble tile. His chest brushes my back, and he traces the shell of my ear with his lips. "Would you try to stop me if I wanted to fuck your ass?" he murmurs, and shivers race down my back.

I close my eyes and turn my face so my cheek is pressed against the wall. "No."

He nips my earlobe, making me jump. "Hmm... Didn't think so." He snakes a hand around me, quickly finding the heat between my legs. Kade rubs my clit in a precise, circular motion before dipping two fingers inside my throbbing pussy. "I think I'll fuck you here, though. You make such lovely noises when I do." He pulls his fingers out and licks them clean before dragging the head of his cock between my ass cheeks. He kicks my legs apart a bit more, and I bite the inside of my cheek, practically vibrating with anticipation.

I brace myself against the wall and pull in a deep breath, but Kade slams into me from behind before I can let it out. "Fucking hell," I gasp.

Kade chuckles darkly, pressing his lips to the side of my neck as he holds still inside me. The walls of my pussy clench and stretch around him, unprepared for the invasion, and my heart pounds against my ribcage. He reaches around to stroke my clit as he pulls back, then slams into me again.

His thrusts are hard and fast. Unrelenting.

I moan, blinking back tears at the intensity of the sensations setting my body ablaze. "Kade," I breathe, my head spinning with lust.

"Fuck," he growls, picking up speed.

Seconds later, he sinks his fangs into my shoulder, and I whimper, my pussy clenching around his cock. He drinks deeply, pounding my pussy and strumming my clit like an instrument. He certainly knows exactly how to play my body to elicit a favorable response.

My chest rises and falls fast, my hardened nipples overly sensitive as they brush the marble tile with each thrust. "Make me come," I pant, tension and pleasure coiling in my stomach. I'm so fucking close.

He pulls back, licking the puncture marks to close them, then flicks my clit hard, shifting the angle of his thrusts to hit a new spot deep inside me, and ignites a world-narrowing orgasm.

I clench around him, coming hard and gasping, reaching

behind me to grab onto him, to hold him against me as I come undone. Hell if I know how I managed to stay upright during that.

Kade pulls out of me, making me shiver with the aftershocks of my orgasm, and turns me around to face him, kissing me softly. "You truly are an angel, aren't you?" he murmurs, his eyes flicking between mine.

"A corrupted one at this point," I tease, sliding my finger along his jaw and kissing him once more. I pull a bottle of body wash off the ledge next to us and squirt some onto my hand, lathering it before I start to wash the remnants of blood off him. I take my time washing everything away, then move onto his hair, because I know how important it is to him under normal circumstances.

Once we're done in the shower, I tug on a robe and guide him out of the bathroom after he's dried off. We walk into the connected bedroom, and I manage to get him into bed without protest. The exhaustion in his eyes makes my chest tighten. He hasn't had a decent rest in far too long.

In that moment, I find myself wishing I could glamour him to close his eyes, forget about everything, and have a restful sleep. But I can't. So I do what I can and pull the blankets up around him, sighing softly.

"Thank you," he says.

I smile. "You're welcome." Resting my hand against his cheek, I say, "Now get some sleep, okay? Please?"

Kade nods.

I pull back and turn to walk out of the bedroom. I'm barely two steps away when Kade's saying my name stops me.

"I haven't loved many people…" he continues, his voice trailing off. I can't bring myself to turn back to him, though I can't figure out why. "I thought maybe I forgot what it felt like. But now I know, each time I look at you, that feeling I used to be so familiar with comes back a little more."

My heart is in my throat and the air gets caught in my lungs. *Fucking breathe. Inhale, then exhale. You've been doing it for twenty-four years. You know how.*

"Calla."

"Kade," I force out, turning enough to look at him over my shoulder.

"Look at me, please. I would very much like to see your face when I tell you that I love you."

I suck in a breath, whirling around to face him with wide eyes. "You just—"

"I love you," he repeats, his lips curling up at the corners.

"I…"

Kade props his hands behind his head against the pillow. "You don't need to say anything. Nothing will change what I've said." He licks his lips, his gaze flicking toward the doorway before returning to me. "You should go back downstairs. Sounds like Gabriel's almost done cooking dinner."

I press my lips together but find myself nodding. "I'll make sure they save you some in case you're hungry later."

He smiles, turning onto his side and settling into the bed. "You're good at taking care of people," he mumbles, his eyes sinking shut.

I step forward and lean over, kissing his forehead gently before walking out of the bedroom, closing the door behind me.

My head is spinning as I fall back against the wall in the hallway outside the bedroom. I press my hand against my chest and feel my heart pounding there.

Kade told me he loves me.

Holy fuck. As if this entire situation with the vampires could get any more complicated.

I've never allowed myself to consider love in connection

with any romantic partner because I knew the fate of my future was sealed. Even now, when it might not be, I'm not sure how to handle the admission.

I care about Kade as much as I do the others. But love? I... I'm not sure I *can*.

In a mixed daze of post-orgasm bliss and confusion, I head back downstairs and run into Atlas on my way to the kitchen. He blocks my path completely, and I am so not in the headspace to battle with him right now. Before I can speak, he steps closer, and I freeze, waiting to see what he's going to do. He leans in and presses his lips against my cheek. "Thank you," he says in a low voice, "for helping Kade."

I step back and nod. "Of course."

"I underestimated you," he admits, his brows pinched.

I blink at him in surprise, not entirely sure what he's making reference to exactly, but manage to recover quickly. "You'd be smart not to do that anymore," I advise him.

He graces me with one of his rare smiles. "Noted."

"'Anymore'?" Lex asks, poking his head into the hallway from the living room. "Does that mean you're staying despite the oath bullshit?"

I walk around Atlas and into the living room, taking the glass of wine Gabriel offers me. I swallow a mouthful and meet Lex's expectant gaze. "Where else am I going to go? There are both vampires and vampire hunters who want to kill me."

Gabriel nods, but there's sadness in his expression. "If you want to go," he says, "we'd ensure you were safe."

I'm still very conflicted over what I want. A month ago, I desperately wanted my freedom, my shot at a future of my choosing, but now... The thought of living a life without the guys makes my chest hurt.

If this is what love feels like, I'm not sure I want it.

❧ 17 ❧
LEX

I'm getting fucking sick of being shaken awake. This time, it's Atlas whose face is right in front of me when I open my eyes. His grim expression makes me shift upright and lean against the headboard. Kade grumbles at the movement from beside me. We fell asleep talking about where we'd go if we can't go back to Washington. We talked about France or Italy, or how lovely it would be to sit pool-side in Bali or Ibiza. The thought of Calla not being there with us, though, made none of the options all that appealing to either of us.

"What the fuck?" Kade growls, covering his head with a pillow as he turns away from us.

I glance at the clock on the small table next to the bed, then arch a brow at Atlas. "It's four in the morning. What's wrong?"

"Downstairs," he says, already heading for the door. "Now."

He's gone before I can say another word, and I sigh. I rake my fingers through my hair and glance over at Kade, whose bare ass is on display. I give it a firm smack and swing my legs over the side of the bed, standing and walking around to his side.

"Fuck off," he says, the sound muffled.

"Come on, get up." I grab his arm and tug on it. "Something's up. We have to see what's going on."

He scowls, turning over and glowering at me. "It's still fucking dark out. What time is it?"

"I don't know," I lie. "Let's go. And put some pants on. I don't think it's the time to be walking around with your dick out."

Kade glances down and shrugs. "You certainly didn't complain about it last night."

I roll my eyes. "Get the fuck up before Atlas loses his shit."

He exhales a dramatic breath. "Fine, fine."

Five minutes later, the five of us are sitting around the living room. Calla is curled up in a blanket on the couch next to Gabriel while he chats softly with Atlas, who is sitting in the armchair across the room.

Kade shuffles into the room and uses the wall to keep himself upright, whereas I lean in the doorway between the hall and living room, wanting to go back to bed as soon as possible. I'd barely gotten an hour of sleep before Atlas woke us.

"Are you going to tell us what's up?" Calla asks around a yawn. Her eyes are squinty, as if she's fighting to keep them open.

"About twenty minutes ago, I received a call from my parents' head advisor. Marcel and several other members of our team have also been in touch. The hunters are fighting back all over North America."

"Fighting back?" Gabriel asks in a tired voice.

Atlas nods. "They're executing counter-attacks against the vampires targeting them. They must have someone feeding them information about the attacks planned against them, because they've become too prepared for them otherwise."

I push away from the doorframe, crossing my arms over my chest as I stand at the back of the couch, looking at Atlas. "Fuck this. It's time to get our hands dirty and enter the fight. Enough is enough. I'm ready to shed some blood and put an end to this."

Gabriel frowns. "I'm not sure that's the best course of action. Diving into the fight now isn't ideal with the other situations we need to work through." He rubs the stubble along his jaw, glancing at each of us for a moment. "That being said, if it comes down to it, we need to protect our own —ourselves and each other."

"Agreed," Atlas says.

"So we're going to sit on the sidelines and see what happens?" Calla says, her brows furrowed.

"We know what happens," Kade chimes in, his chin nearly touching his chest as he keeps his gaze on the floor. "When you live forever, history tends to repeat itself. Once in a while, the hunters get on some power trip and think they can eliminate the vampires. They ignore the long-standing history between us. Never have they succeeded in their mission to rid the world of us—obviously—and they won't."

"And they never fucking learn," I say, irritation making my tone sharp. Not that anytime the hunters decide they can overpower us in numbers and strength is a particularly convenient time, but now—with everything coming up about the blood oath and trying to hunt Selene—is pretty much the worst possible timing to have to deal with hunters trying to punch outside their weight class.

"Does this mean we still can't go back to Washington?" Calla asks.

"No," Atlas says. "We'll go home today."

Huh. That's news to me.

Her eyes widen. "Wait, really?"

"Why now?" Kade follows up, his head tipped back against the wall now. He appears as exhausted as the rest of us, though some of the darkness in his eyes has faded, which makes me feel slightly better. I'm still worried about him, but I think Calla's strength got through to him last night. And I am beyond grateful for that.

"Lenora and Simon believe we're here because of Gabriel's sire. Knowing them, they are attempting to verify that. If we stay longer, they're sure to figure out we lied about our reason for being here."

"God forbid," Calla mutters tiredly.

"You wouldn't be saying that if you knew them," I comment mildly. Atlas's parents are some of the most powerful and vicious vampires to exist. They have no regard for human life and believe their son should share the same view. If they found out we came here for Calla to see her parents... I don't think any of us want to see what would happen in that instance.

She sighs. "Whatever. If we're going back to Washington, I want to see Brighton."

"We'll discuss how we are going to deal with Miss Ellis once we're home," Atlas says in a voice that leaves no room for further questions, much less argument.

Calla frowns at him but doesn't push it.

"While we're all here," Gabriel says, crossing one leg over the other and resting his ankle atop the opposing knee.

"Does it have to be now, Gabe?" I say, my brows pinching together. "Can we at least make a pot of coffee first?" It's clear we're not going back to bed, so might as well try to bring myself somewhat to life with a shot of caffeine.

"I'll do it," Calla says quickly, pulling herself off the couch and keeping the blanket wrapped around her shoulders. She can't get out of the room fast enough.

I have the itch to reach for her as she passes me, but I force myself to focus on Gabriel.

He scratches his jaw. "Fallon and Jase have been keeping tabs on Selene in Chicago, but the longer they wait to make a move while they continue tracking her, the bigger chance there is that she's going to figure out she's being watched."

"Lex and I can meet up with them in Chicago while you and Kade take Calla back to Washington," Atlas says.

Calla pokes her head back into the room, her eyes narrowed at Atlas. "Absolutely not."

He draws in a slow breath, turning his attention to her. "Want to try that again?"

She crosses her arms. "I said, no, Atlas. I know you're not familiar with the word, having heard it on so few occasions, but I would've thought you'd be used to it from me by now."

The corners of his mouth twitch ever so slightly. The movement is brief, barely enough to catch; Calla likely missed it. "Careful," he warns, his silver gaze sharp and the tips of his fangs visible. If I had to bet, he hasn't fed in a while, and Calla seems to taunt the monster in him—in all of us, really. And as dangerous as it is, the allure is near impossible to ignore.

Calla doesn't flinch. "We need to stay together," she argues. "I don't want you sending them with me for protection or whatever when the two of you are going after that psychopath." She shakes her head and repeats herself in a firmer tone. "*No.*"

The coffee machine gurgles from the kitchen, and Calla retreats once more, presumably to get some coffee.

I turn my attention to my sire. "I'm on board for Chicago. I say let's go and deal with the bitch. We can certainly take her out without these two." I jerk my thumb toward Kade, then Gabriel. "No offense."

"Fucker," Kade mutters under his breath halfheartedly,

and Gabriel says nothing. He wouldn't be able to do anything against Selene even if he wanted to.

Calla returns to the living room with a steaming mug of coffee and lowers herself back onto the couch. We're all watching her as she takes a small sip and sets the mug on the coffee table in front of her before settling into the cushions. A moment later, she realizes and scrunches her nose up in an annoyingly cute way I can't ignore. "What?" she mumbles, her cheeks turning pink under our gazes.

"We will all go to Washington," Atlas says to Calla, then turns to Gabriel. "I imagine Fallon and Jase have backup if necessary?"

Gabriel nods.

"Good." Atlas stands. "Give them the order to kill Selene by whatever means necessary."

My chest tightens and disappointment flows through me. "I thought we were going to take her out."

He shrugs. "It's not worth the hassle of us all going to Chicago to deal with her when there are already people we trust there that can handle it."

I frown at him but don't say anything further. I was ready to fight, to punish the vampire who tortured Calla and had her hooks in Gabriel so deep for decades, but Atlas was quick to concede to Calla's wish that we all stay together. She is changing all of us in different ways—even big, bad, powerful Atlas York, and I'm not even sure he realizes it.

After we've packed, we head to the airstrip and board the York family private jet, courtesy of Atlas's mother and father. The interior is all black leather and dark wood. It smells mildly of lavender and sage, no doubt cleaned pristinely just before we boarded.

Kade drops onto the couch in the middle of the plane, keeping his sunglasses on and crossing his arms over his chest as he stretches his legs out. In minutes, before the plane has even taken off, he's asleep. As jealous as I am, I'm glad he's getting rest. He needs it the most of all of us right now. That, and an escape from reality, even just for a little while.

Gabriel and Atlas sit across from each other near the front of the plane, drinking what looks and smells like whiskey from crystal glasses and speaking softly about future plans to return to the house we built in the Palisades. It may be a far-off goal, but I'm looking forward to returning to the only place I've ever felt like home, and I think the others share my sentiment.

I guide Calla to the back of the plane, sitting next to her as she starts reading something on her phone. She seems content to pretend I'm not here, but I'm in the mood to mess with her a bit.

"Whatcha reading?" I ask in a light tone, leaning in until my shoulder brushes hers and peering at the screen.

"A book." She turns it away from me without a word as the plane taxis to the runway.

"Oh, come on. Let me see," I drag out the word. "I won't judge." The plane engine powers up, vibrating the cabin, and a moment later, we accelerate down the runway.

Calla huffs out a laugh as we ascend into the air. "Judge all you want, Lex. I really don't care."

"Tell me what you're reading then," I challenge, shooting her a wink. "Oooh, is it a dirty book?"

She rolls her eyes. "You are insufferable."

"Hmm." I lower my voice, speaking softly into her ear. "Will you say that after I make you come in that chair?"

"What?" she squeaks, her pulse jumping.

I smirk at her. "Want to join the mile high club?" The race of her heart and the flush of her cheeks tells me all I need to know. I lean in, dragging my tongue along her neck before pressing a kiss against the pulse point at her throat. Her breath catches, and I slide my hand up her thigh, teasingly slow.

"Lex," she says, her voice strained.

I press my finger against her lips. "Shh." Reaching for the seat belt, I move at a speed too quick for her to track and use the material to secure her wrists to the armrests. She immediately tries tugging on them to free herself, but the woven strap—and my handiwork—is too strong to break.

"What are you doing?" she asks, glancing down at her restraints before looking up at me.

"Making sure you don't move," I tell her, giving a quick pull on the seat belt to make sure it's secure.

Her eyes narrow. "Let me go."

I purse my lips, shaking my head. "Go where? We're over thirty thousand feet in the air."

She holds my gaze, looking rather unimpressed. "You know that's not what I mean."

I get up from my chair and lean over hers, close enough our noses nearly touch. "Why would I let you go when I could do this instead?" I trail two fingers down the center of her chest slowly, heading toward her navel and keeping my eyes locked with hers. She swallows, her breath hitching when I reach the waistband of her dark gray joggers. Without hesitation, I slide my hand into her panties, brushing the soft, delicate skin of her folds. She catches her bottom lip between her teeth, tipping her head back against the seat, then lets out an uneven breath.

"Calla?" I murmur, my lips tracing the shell of her ear.

"What?" she grumbles through her teeth.

My lips curve into a grin. "Do you want my fingers inside you?"

Instead of answering me, she arches her hips, causing the tips of my fingers to dip between her folds.

I pull my hand out of her panties. "Ah, ah, ah."

She exhales a frustrated sigh. "Stop tormenting me."

"But it's so much fun," I counter in a voice laced with amusement. Playing with her is the highest level of entertainment I've found in a long time. Even better, I know she enjoys it just as much as I do, whether she admits it or not. I tease her over her joggers, sliding my hand between her thighs and tracing the outline of her panties before pressing my thumb against her clit.

Calla sucks in a sharp breath. "Fine. You're so determined to hear me say the words? I want you to fuck me with your fingers, your tongue, your cock—whatever. Just *fuck me*."

"So impatient," I tsk.

She glowers at me. "I know what I want and I'm not afraid to ask for it. Now fuck me or leave me alone to read my book in peace."

"Fine," I say, "but first I want to show you something." I grab my duffle bag off the chair across the aisle.

"Oh, god." She sighs. "Do I even want to know?"

I chuckle. "Let's find out."

She arches a brow at me but stays silent.

Unzipping the bag, I reach in and search for the box Kade and I picked up before we left Monroe. "We picked this up for your birthday and then forgot to give it to you. Apologies, it's not wrapped."

"Um, okay. I thought the tattoo was my birthday present. I don't need—"

I pull out the box and set it in her lap, grinning as her cheeks turn pink when she sees the dark purple vibrating dildo. "I'm sure you'll find a use for it."

"You give me gifts like this, and I might not have a need for you."

"Sure," I remark dryly. "I'm not worried. I don't see sex toys as my enemy. If anything, they're amazing teammates."

"Right, okay. Cool. Not sure how I'm supposed to use this when you've tied my wrists to the seat, but thanks?"

I take the box back, popping it open and sliding out the toy. "Allow me." I toss the box aside and lift the dildo to her mouth. "Open."

Her eyes widen, and she hesitates, but eventually she does as I say. I slide the toy along her tongue, and she closes her lips around it, making my cock twitch in my pants, imagining her doing that to me. I pull it out of her mouth, and it's shiny with her saliva.

"Good girl," I say in a low voice. "Now lift your hips."

She plants her feet on the ground and arches forward enough for me to pull her joggers and panties down to her knees. The moment her ass is planted back in the seat, I have the dildo between her legs, vibrating against her clit.

"Shit," she hisses, her lips parting in a soundless gasp.

I spread her legs as wide as they'll go in the chair and drag the head of the toy along her slit, turning the vibration higher with each pass.

She pulls against the restraints, glaring at me as I tease her over and over. I'm sure I'll pay for it later, but right now it's just too damn good to resist.

I turn down the vibration a bit and push the tip of the dildo inside her pussy. Her muscles tense, and she presses her lips together. I slide it deeper, using my other hand to circle her clit slowly, and when I start to pull it out, she closes her thighs, holding it inside her.

"Don't you dare," she practically growls, her chest rising and falling a little quicker than normal.

I push it in deeper, making her suck in a shallow breath. "Better?" I ask smugly, twisting it and turning up the vibration.

She nods quickly, her hips arching as I pull it back slightly before thrusting it deeper once more, eliciting a sweet moan from her lips.

"So responsive," I murmur. "I should tie you up more often."

"More," she demands, ignoring my taunt.

I pick up the speed of my thrusts, again increasing the intensity of the vibration, and Calla gasps sharply, her eyes closing as her head falls back against the seat, and she tugs on the restraints. My thumb circles her clit hard and fast, and her thighs shake as an orgasm washes over her. She grips the armrests until her knuckles are white and presses her lips together in a feeble attempt to quiet her moans.

I pull the vibrator out of her, switching it off and tossing it onto the chair across the aisle. Before she can open her eyes, I slam my mouth against hers, kissing her deeply and gripping her chin to hold her to me. She responds immediately, kissing me back with fervor and breathing heavily into my mouth. I lean back and undo the restraints. She immediately grabs the front of my shirt, drawing me back to her mouth, and we kiss once more. Her tongue dances along mine before retreating, and I nip her bottom lip playfully.

As I'm dropping back into my seat, Atlas saunters over with his fangs bared, likely having smelled Calla's arousal. I can tell by the look in his eyes, though, he doesn't want to fuck her at this very moment. He wants her blood.

Without a word, Atlas grabs her wrist and pulls her out of the chair. Her jaw is set tight, her eyes roaming over his face as he guides her toward the other couch opposite to where Kade is asleep. He sits, pulling her onto his lap, and she steadies herself by grabbing his shoulders. She licks her lips, and Atlas's eyes drop to her mouth, darkening. Calla moves her hair over one shoulder, exposing her neck and tilting her head to the side as she leans in, pressing her chest against his.

His hands go to her hips, settling her in his lap, and I watch with fascination as they seem to communicate without words before Atlas sinks his fangs into her throat.

Calla makes a short sound of discomfort before her tense expression relaxes, and she sighs softly, leaning fully into Atlas as he closes his eyes and drinks deeply. The pounding of her heart slows as the seconds tick by, and when Atlas pulls away from her neck, he shifts her off his lap and onto the couch. She slumps back against the armrest, a look of serenity overcoming her features.

Atlas gets up as Gabriel comes to sit with her, putting his arm around her shoulders and guiding her to rest against his side.

The smell of her blood in the air makes my fangs slice through my gums, and I lick my lips. As much as I want to drink her blood—as much as the monster that craves her warmth and her life is pushing me to take from her—I hold myself back. We don't need her passing out before we land in Washington.

Instead, I get up and walk to the front of the plane, grabbing a blood bag from the mini fridge at the bar, hoping it'll be enough to sate the monster for now.

❧ 18 ❧
CALLA

When we touch down in Washington, there's a black town car waiting at the private airstrip. The four of us pile into the back while Atlas takes the passenger seat, speaking in a low voice to the driver.

In minutes, we're on the road, and I stare out the window at the familiar buildings and signs, wondering if we'll end up at another safe house.

When we pull up outside the hotel Brighton had booked a room for me on the night I tried to escape the guys, I shake my head. The others don't seem to notice, but when we get out of the car, I shoot Atlas a look, knowing he would have been the one to arrange this, to which he offers me a quick smile.

The bastard actually made sure we got the exact suite I'd stayed in, and while the four of them sit in the dining room area, I slip away to the bedroom to check in with my parents. I call my dad's phone in case Mom is resting and I'm surprised when she's the one who picks up. "Oh hey, Mom. How are you doing?"

"Calla, sweetie. I'm doing well, all things considered."

"Yeah?" I check. A tinge of worry still lingering in me. I wish I'd gotten to see her again before we left the city, but once the hunter situation is dealt with, I tell myself, I'll go back to New York and have a proper visit with them. Part of me wants to ask if Dad told her about the oath and about me finding out about the baby, but I can't bring myself to say the words. So I say, "We're back in Washington."

"That's good, honey. So exams must be coming up, right?"

I bite my lip, wondering how I should go about telling her that I didn't finish the semester. "Yeah, I'm actually taking a brief pause on school. Things got very complicated way too quickly for me to keep up with everything." That has nothing to do with school and everything to do with the chaos that my life has become in a matter of a couple months.

"Calla—"

"Mom, I know. I don't want you to worry. School is still my priority. I'm not going to drop out—I will graduate, I promise you."

"I'm just worried about you, that's all."

"I called to check in on *you*."

"Yeah, well, we did me. I'm good. Now let me worry about my daughter. It's natural for a mother, okay?"

"Things are... fine," I tell her, surprised to find my chin wobbling and my vision blurring. I want to confide in my mom, to hear her advice on what I should do about the guys, about Brighton, about Kade telling me he loved me—about *everything,* and yet instead I say, "I won't keep you. I just wanted to make sure you were still doing good."

"Calla, why do I feel like there's something you want to say but aren't?"

"There are things I want to say that I *can't*," I tell her, which is mostly true. "But I should be able to tell you soon, I hope."

"I don't even want to ask this, but are those boys taking care of you?"

I press my lips together. "Mom, I don't think you can call them *boys* when they're significantly older than you."

She sighs. "I try not to think about it that way, to be honest."

"Yeah, you and me both. Listen, I should go but I'll check in with you soon, okay?"

"All right, sweetheart. Know that I love you."

"I know. I love you too."

After ending the call with my mom, my finger hovers over Brighton's name, and I fight the urge to call her. I want to reach out to her, to meet up with her now that we're back in the city. I think a face-to-face conversation would do a lot more than speaking over the phone or by text. More than that, I want to hug my best friend.

I chew my thumb, staring at the screen, and then my fingers are moving. I open a new text and ask her to meet, knowing that one if not all of the guys might actually kill me for this. I pace the bedroom until her response comes in a few minutes later. And then I sit on the end of the bed, reading it over three times.

Calla, I'm so sorry for how things went the last time we spoke. It wasn't fair what I asked you to do and I feel like I'm losing my mind.

I sniffle, blinking back tears, because I understand that completely. And I want to go to her but I know the guys will never allow that in a million years. So instead of trying to keep it from them, I walk back out to the living room catching Gabriel's gaze.

"Go for a walk with me? I could use some fresh air."

We head down to the lobby, but before the elevator reaches the ground floor, Gabriel pushes the emergency stop.

"Is there something you want to tell me, angel?" he asks in

a gentle tone, his expression open, willing me to confide in him.

"Yes," I answer honestly. "I've been in contact with Brighton—just today. Not that long ago when we were upstairs. I want to meet up with her and make sure she's okay, but I knew if I tried to do that without telling you guys it wouldn't go over very well."

Gabriel presses lips together and nods slowly, leaning against the elevator wall. "Thank you for trusting me enough to bring this to me. And, Calla, I understand your concern for your friend, but we can't help her. Not only will interfering with Scott's daughter bring more unwanted attention on us, Brighton hates vampires for what happened to her mom. And rightfully so. But there will never be enough trust between us to make whatever you're thinking or hoping work."

I bite down on my bottom lip to keep it from trembling as tears burn my eyes. I never thought the day would come where I was torn between my best friend and them. I open my mouth to respond, but Gabriel's phone chimes.

He pulls it out and frowns. "It's Atlas. We need to get back upstairs."

My stomach drops, and I shake my head. "What, why? What's going on?"

He hits another button, making the elevator start moving again. "There's an attack happening on a community of vampires on the university campus." The elevator reaches the lobby, and we take it back up to our floor.

Back in the room, Atlas, Kade, and Lex are scrambling around, getting changed and drinking the blood bags we brought from the plane.

I tie my hair back and down half a bottle of water, trying to calm my nerves.

"I called Marcel. He's sending two of his guys to stay here with you," Lex says.

I bark out a choked laugh. "What the fuck did you just say? I'm going with you."

"You should stay behind, angel," Gabriel says softly.

I ignore him, my eyes falling on Atlas, and I can see the debate happening in his expression. He's considering glamouring me into submission. I hold his gaze, daring him to do it. My narrowed eyes tell him that I will be beyond livid if he goes through with it.

When he steps forward, I force myself to stand my ground. He stops right in front of me, wrapping his hand around my thigh, touching the dagger there. His eyes travel the length of my body as he leans in, his breath tickling my cheek. His jaw is set tight, his eyes dark and serious. "Look at me."

I do despite the fact his words hold no weight of glamour. The intensity of his gaze burns right through me.

"You do not hesitate, you understand me?"

My eyes widen as my pulse jumps. I swallow hard past the dryness in my throat. I'm not exactly sure I can kill humans but I find myself nodding anyway.

Everything happens so quickly. We're in the car, speeding towards campus in the dark. I don't immediately see chaos when we arrive, but the moment we get out of the car, I hear the sounds of battle and my blood runs cold.

Our group rushes toward the fight, Lex and Kade on one side of me, and Gabriel and Atlas on the other. We round the corner of one of the buildings and nearly trip over a female vampire trying to flee, with blood-soaked clothes and wide silver eyes. She appears weak and scared and young—so fucking young it makes my chest ache. Gabriel stops her, making sure she's relatively unharmed before letting her go. She disappears in a blur of movement a moment later.

Once we get close enough, I notice there's a large group of people, some moving in blurs of shapes and others trying to tear them down with guns and daggers.

The guys dive into the fight, whereas I stay near the outside. I'm not so arrogant I think I can dodge a bullet at close range. My eyes fall on a wounded vampire several feet away. There's a dagger sticking out of his chest, but he's still moving. I race over to him, darting around several hunters covered in blood, whether it be their own or that of a vampire, I can't tell in the dark. I fall to the ground at the vampire's side and pull the stake out of his chest.

He coughs up blood, and it spatters across his cheek. His eyes widen when he realizes I'm human. "Why… are you helping me?" he says in a broken voice.

"I'm not with them," I insist. "I'm not a hunter." I toss the dagger far enough away he won't be worried I'm going to stab him with it.

"It scraped my heart. It's going to take me too long to heal. There are too many hunters…" His voice trails off as fear fills his dirt and bloodstained features.

My eyes don't leave his face. If he doesn't heal and get out of here, it's very possible that another hunter will come for him. So I do something potentially stupid and offer him my wrist. "Don't take too much," I warn him. "There are four very scary vampires here who will actually kill you if you hurt me."

There's no hesitation in his movements. He grabs my wrist, and I see a flash of his fangs before he sinks them into my skin. It doesn't hurt as much as I was expecting it to. Maybe it's because I gave myself willingly.

A moment later, I cringe when I hear Atlas shout, "For the love of god, Calla," and I know I'm going to pay for this act of kindness on my part later.

The vampire on the ground pulls away from my wrist,

and I cover it with my palm. I help him up, and he offers me a grateful smile before he disappears into the night. I turn and come face-to-face with Atlas.

"Are you fucking kidding me?" he growls, fangs bared.

"We don't have time for this," I mutter. "I helped him. It's fine. Get over it."

His eyes are ablaze with pure fury. "Do you know how many vampires are around right now?"

"Yes, and we're trying to help them, so quit being jealous someone else had my blood and—"

"Enough. Do that again, and I will drag you back to the car myself and make sure you stay there. Don't give me that look. I don't take too kindly to others having what's mine." It goes without saying that Gabriel, Lex, and Kade are the exception.

Heat floods through me, stealing my breath at his possessiveness. I don't know if I want to kiss him or punch him, and we really don't have time for either.

He rips the dagger out of its holder at my thigh and shoves it into my hand. "A lot of good it does you there. Hang on to this. Use it and—" His voice cuts off, and he sighs, muttering a curse under his breath.

I shake my head, searching his face. "What? Why is your face like that?"

A muscle ticks in his jaw. "You're going to be upset with this."

"I mean, add it to the list. What is it, Atlas?"

"Your friend is here."

"What?" I turn and find Brighton fighting alongside the hunters, her father not too far away in a white dress shirt spattered with blood. While it's clear to me the hunters are severely outnumbered, clearly it's not so much to them, because they continue fighting.

Brighton's eyes turn to me and widen. She shakes her

head, abandoning the attack she was carrying out. Tears fill her eyes, and I charge forward, ignoring any and all caution as I stomp through the battle, with Atlas at my side. Except, I'm not heading for Brighton. My sights are set on Scott.

"Are you ready to do this now?" Atlas asks. He knows exactly what I need to do.

"I don't know," I admit, his words catching me up as we continue toward them.

"Calla, what are you doing?" Brighton asks, panic filling her eyes, and I barely hear her. I want to be understanding of her being here, I really fucking do, but right now, I can't find the grace to grant her that. And there's not a chance in hell of finding it for her father.

Scott finally sees me, recognition flaring to life in his gaze.

"You fucking monster," I seethe before he can say anything to me. "You put your own daughter in danger to settle some score?"

"That's not what's happening!" Brighton attempts to denounce my claim with tears in her eyes. I have no clue why or *how* she's standing there defending her father. "I'm fighting for my mom, Calla."

I shake my head, flinching at the sound of a pain-filled scream from somewhere behind me, and keep my eyes on my best friend, the desperation in her gaze no doubt reflected in mine. "It was your mom who fought so hard to keep you out of this fight, Bri. She didn't want this life for you, remember?" It was never a secret that she wanted to keep Brighton out of the family business—the secret had been what the business *was*.

Scott grabs Brighton's arm, but I grab the other before he can pull her away from me. "You don't have to go with him. *Please* don't go with him," I implore her, knowing at that moment and despite the dagger clenched in my other hand, I won't be able to kill Scott myself. As desperate as I am to avenge what he did to my mom, I can't do that to Brighton. Seeing her like this now, I'm not sure she would survive it.

From my peripheral, I catch a quick glance at Atlas helping a couple of vampires who are being ganged up on by half a dozen hunters. He moves with a lethal grace, striking them down with his bare hands in a matter of seconds.

Brighton sniffles, snapping my attention back to her as tears roll down her cheeks, and she lowers her voice. "He's my dad, Calla. He's all I have left."

My heart cleaves in two, and I shake my head, letting go of her wrist. "All you have?" I whisper, betrayal whipping through me like ice in my veins, and I struggle to hold her gaze.

Scott clears his throat and pulls Brighton away from me. "It's time to go."

"Don't," I warn her, my eyes wide as I stare at her and my grip tightening on my dagger, as if I could use it to keep her with me. "If you go, you're dead. They *will* kill you—I won't be able to stop them."

"She's dead if she stays," Scott hisses, tightening his grip on the dagger in the hand he doesn't have wrapped around Brighton's arm.

"You started this," I growl at him, my voice sharp and filled with venom. "You're severely outnumbered here, Scott. You brought your daughter into this, and—"

"Brighton," he cuts me off, blatantly ignoring my presence. Brighton gives me one last tear-filled look before she turns and runs toward the parking lot with her father.

I can barely see, my eyes overflowing with tears. I stumble back, nearly tripping over a body. I'm not sure whether it's a vampire or hunter. The numbers are dwindling and there's death on both sides. But there's a sick part of me that's glad Scott got away only because it means Brighton is safe.

I don't try to stop them, because if we kill Scott, they'll kill Brighton too. I try to blink the tears away, but they fall down my cheeks, and I wipe my face with the back of my hand, sniffling as my nose runs. My eyes fall on Kade, who looks near demonic in battle.

Something in him has snapped, I realize with a tightness in my chest that makes it hard to breathe.

He's ripping through hunters too quickly for them to even attempt to fight back. He notices Scott and Brighton getting away and starts toward them.

A strangled cry gets stuck in my throat, and Atlas pulls him back.

I rush toward them as Kade fights Atlas's grip, gnashing his bloody fangs in Atlas's face. "Kade!" I scream, my voice cracking with pain.

His eyes swing toward me, and he blinks, then stops fighting Atlas. "Calla—"

"Please," I force out through my tears, "just... let them go. *Please.*"

His jaw hardens, his gaze lowering for a moment before meeting mine. "Okay," he finally says, stepping away from Atlas and toward me. His nostrils flare, and he frowns. "You're bleeding."

"No, I... Well, yeah. I'm okay, though." He must've been too wrapped up in his lust for hunter blood he didn't realize when Atlas did that I'd fed that vampire.

Atlas keeps his eyes locked on Kade for a moment before they flick to me. A second later, he moves in a blur and reenters the fight. Scott and Brighton might've fled, but other hunters are still determined to spill vampire blood tonight.

Gabriel is the farthest away, helping another vampire to

his feet, and Lex howls in delight, tearing into a hunter's throat and spraying blood on the lawn.

I cringe at the vicious sight as Kade moves around me to follow Atlas back into battle.

Between one moment and the next, hands wrap around my shoulders from behind and I'm flying toward the ground. I don't have time to put my hands out and catch my fall. I land hard on my hip, and pain explodes along my side. Before I have a second to recover, I'm flipped over and end up face-to-face with a very pissed off vampire, his fangs snapping way too close for comfort.

"Hunter," he snarls in my face.

"I'm not! Get… off of… me," I hiss, struggling beneath the dark-haired vampire. His mouth is already covered with blood, and I cringe as it drips onto my face. My stomach roils as his fangs get closer to my throat, and panic claws into me as I reach around desperately. I wrap my fingers around the dagger at my thigh, pulling it out of its holder and gripping it tightly. I try again to shove him off, but he growls in my face, slamming me hard against the ground. I cry out, my vision blurring, and he presses his body into me, sinking his fangs into my shoulder.

My muscles tense, and I yelp in pain. Something in me snaps, and I use every ounce of strength I have to thrust my arm up, sinking the dagger into the vampire's chest. I have no idea if I hit his heart, but he reels back and falls to the ground beside me.

Gabriel is there, pulling me off the ground and holding me upright, while Lex pulls the vampire up and tears into his throat so hard his head rolls off his neck and lands in the grass with a sickening *thump*.

I turn away, pressing my face into Gabriel's chest as nausea rolls through me like a vicious wave. Pain radiates through my whole body as blood seeps through my shirt.

Consciousness threatens to slip away from me, my vision dimming around the edges, and I fight to cling to it.

"Calla," Gabriel says, supporting the majority of my weight; I'm far too unsteady to stand on my own. "Keep your eyes open. You're okay, angel. Everything is going to be okay."

I don't feel okay.

The sounds of pained and angry shouts grows quieter as Gabriel guides me away from what's left of the fight, while Lex rejoins Kade and Atlas, striking down more hunters with dangerous ease. Sirens blare in the distance; we don't have much time to get out of here before the authorities arrive.

"Did I kill that vampire?" I force out, trying to look back to where his decapitated body landed in the grass.

"Lex did," Gabriel answers in a gentle voice.

My brows pull together and even that hurts. "So I... I didn't hit his heart?"

"No, you didn't."

Relief floods through me. Sure, he still ended up dead, but not by my hand. I'm glad I was able to defend myself, but if anything, this reaffirmed that I'm not ready to kill anyone. I'm not sure I'll ever be ready for that.

Things seem to end quite quickly after that, or maybe I just go numb. I'm not really sure. By the time Gabriel and I make it to the car, the others have joined us.

Atlas immediately crowds my personal space and snags my chin, tipping my head back and looking into my eyes. "You forgot something."

I squint at him through the pain pounding in my head. "What?"

He holds up my dagger, still covered in that vampire's blood. After wiping it off on his shirt, he returns it to the holder at my thigh and leans in until his lips are at my ear. "You did good."

My stomach flutters despite the pain radiating from the rest of me. Atlas is proud of me and that's doing weird things to my heart. I lean back a little to look at him, and my stance falters. He catches me around the waist, holding me against his chest.

"Calla." His voice sounds far away.

Darkness crowds my vision again and my ears start ringing. Shit. How hard did I hit my head?

"Calla?" Atlas's face blurs in front of me. "Fuck. Lex, you drive." He tosses the keys before sweeping my feet off the ground and cradling me against his chest as he gets into the car.

Gabriel is in the seat beside us. "She needs—"

"I know," Atlas cuts him off, looking down at me.

My chest tightens at the worry in his eyes. I'm not entirely sure what he's referring to. I want to suggest a doctor or a hospital maybe, but I have a feeling that's not where we're going.

The movement of the car doesn't help matters, and I squeeze my eyes shut, clenching my jaw so I don't whimper in pain.

"Calla, I know you're in pain, but I need you to look at me."

I manage to pry my eyes open enough to see Atlas's face.

"There you are," he murmurs in a voice so soft it nearly doesn't sound like him. "Listen to me. I'm going to take the pain away, all right?"

"Wha—?" Realization hits me, and I groan. "No."

Something like a tinge of reserved amusement passes over his features. "You can complain all you want and try to stab me later, but this is what's happening."

I narrow my eyes. I want to pull away from him, but there's not a shot in hell I have the strength for that.

Atlas lifts his arm, and I see a flash of his fangs before

they're in his wrist. A second later, he pulls it back. "Are you going to make this difficult?"

After glaring at him for a good ten seconds, I shake my head. The thought of drinking his blood makes me all hot and panicky, but the pain and blood loss I'm experiencing outweigh that—barely.

"Good. You can close your eyes if that'll help."

I wet my lips, managing to lift my hands and cradle his wrist in them. He brings it to my mouth, and my pulse kicks up the moment before I close my lips around the blood pooling on his skin. My eyes flutter shut as his blood coats my tongue, warming my stomach as it glides down my throat. Almost immediately, the pain fades. The pounding behind my eyes and the pain in my side is gone. The skin around where the vampire bit my shoulder tingles, healing as Atlas's blood flows through me.

He pulls his wrist away from my mouth, and I think I shock both of us when I lick my lips, because what the hell? Why am I acting like I want *more*?

I drop my gaze, trying to ignore the heat flaring in my cheeks. "I... um, thanks."

He nods and helps me sit up but makes no move to shift me off his lap.

We're back at the hotel shortly thereafter. The guys glamour anybody who sees us on our way back to the suite, considering we look like we just participated in a massacre, which I suppose we did.

The guys take turns showering the blood off of them and they collectively decide to toss their clothes. When it's my turn for the shower, Lex offers to help, but I wave him off, needing a minute to myself.

I stand under the hot spray of water, letting it mix with my tears and the blood rinsing off my skin.

Tonight is a turning point. Brighton has made her choice, and I think… I feel that I've made mine.

We're on opposite sides of a war that neither of us should have to be involved in, and I'm not really sure how to deal with that right now.

After my shower, I wrap myself in the plush hotel robe and walk back out to the main living space. Gabriel's in the kitchen with Kade where they're sipping on glasses of whiskey.

Atlas is on his phone, speaking quickly and with a grim expression on his face, likely reporting back to somebody in New York who will relay whatever message he gives to his super scary, super powerful vampire parents.

Lex is lying on the couch, watching some trashy reality show.

We sure are a sight to be seen.

I perch myself on the armrest of the couch, vaguely paying attention to the TV, but not really able to focus on the drama unfolding. Not when I have so much of it in my real life.

Lex sits up as Gabriel and Kade come into the room and says, "We all need to decompress. I think we should have a game night."

I groan. "My god, Lex. Please don't say—"

"I think we need to do it. I think we really do need to play strip poker."

"What is with your fixation on this game?" Gabriel asks.

"I don't know, man. I just think it would be fun. Plus, I'm really fucking good at poker."

Kade says nothing, which concerns me, especially after seeing him in battle tonight. He catches me looking at him and arches eyebrow at me as if to ask why I'm watching him. I arch one right back, to which he smirks faintly, shaking his head and downing the rest of his drink. "If we're doing this," he says, "I'm going to need another drink."

"I'm going to need several," I mutter.

"Strip poker?" Gabriel is looking at Lex. "Really?"

Lex grins and nods, looking like a kid on Christmas morning who was told he would be going to Disney World.

An hour later, the five of us are in various stages of undress in the living room of our hotel suite. I'm on the couch with Kade, while Lex sits on the floor with his back against the couch, and Gabriel and Atlas are occupying the armchairs opposite us.

"You know," I say to Lex, trying and failing to suppress a wry smile as I run my fingers through the back of his hair, "for the guy who has been so insistent on playing strip poker, you kinda suck at this game. So much for being 'really fucking good at poker,' huh?"

He grumbles something under his breath that I don't quite catch, snatching one of the decorative pillows from the couch to cover his crotch.

"Now don't be a poor sport, Lex," Kade says, taking a drink of his whiskey and blood cocktail before setting the glass on the coffee table. I've gotten fairly skilled at mixing alcohol and blood tonight. I'm also apparently quite good at poker, considering I'm still wearing my T-shirt, bra, and panties. Kade is down to his boxers, as is Gabriel, and Atlas has only lost his jacket, shirt, and shoes. Because *of course* he's also good at poker.

"I have a better game," Kade offers, angling himself toward me.

I arch a brow at him. "Oh? Another one that will leave poor Lex in his birthday suit I hope?"

Kade smirks, running his hand up my bare thigh and making my skin tingle under his touch. "That's the idea. Though you, my sweet and fiery Calla, are still wearing entirely too much clothing." He slides his finger along my hip, under my panties, and tears them clear off me before I have a second to protest, dropping them in Lex's lap.

My cheeks flush hotly, and I narrow my eyes at him. "Your game is to ruin my clothes?"

He catches my chin, leaning in until his lips nearly touch mine, and my senses are overwhelmed by a mixture of citrus and whiskey and Kade. "My game is to see which of us can make you come the hardest."

Holy fuck.

My pulse cranks way up, pounding like a jackhammer beneath my skin, and my throat goes dry.

The corner of his mouth kicks up, and he says, "I thought that might pique your interest." His mouth is on mine before I can respond, his tongue teasing my lips and coaxing them open until they part and he pushes into my mouth. Our tongues dance as I lean into him, my eyes shut and my stomach fluttering like a jar filled with butterflies. When he pulls me onto his lap and his erection presses between my thighs through his boxers, I gasp against his lips. He grips my hips, and they instinctively start moving, seeking to address the growing friction at my core.

Lex shifts behind me, his chest against my back as he leans in to press his lips against my shoulder. He slides his hands under my shirt and bra, cupping my breasts and tweaking my nipples into stiff peaks.

I moan into Kade's mouth, grinding harder against his erection. I slide my fingers into his unbelievably soft hair, gripping the back of it, and reach between us with my free hand, palming the bulge in his boxers. He stiffens and groans against my lips, nipping my bottom one with his teeth.

"Keep moving like that," he says in a low voice, "and I'm going to fuck you so hard the game will be over before it even starts."

I rest my forehead against his, catching my breath. "Still sounds like a win to me."

Lex presses his lips just below my ear, his tongue darting out and teasing the sensitive skin there. "Not before I have a chance to devour you again." He pinches my nipples, and I yelp in surprise more than pain. He pulls his hands out of my shirt, then promptly pulls it up and off over my head. I turn in time to see him toss it toward Gabriel, who shakes his head, grinning faintly as he watches us.

"Fear not. You'll have your turn, brother," Lex tells him.

"I certainly hope so," he says, holding my gaze, and I smile, biting my lip as my face warms.

Kade's grip on my hips tightens, pulling my attention back to him. He slides me off his lap, laying me across the couch with my back against his bare chest, and Lex grabs one of my ankles, pulling it over the edge until my foot touches the floor and I'm spread open for him. My breath catches in my throat as he licks his lips, his gaze locked between my thighs, filled with a hunger that makes me shiver. He kisses from just below my knee all the way up my thigh, and the moment his lips brush my folds, I sigh, tipping my head back against Kade's shoulder. He kisses my cheek, snaking his arm around my waist, securing me to him as Lex licks the length of my slit.

"Fuck," I breathe, closing my eyes as pleasure floods through me and warmth fills my stomach.

Kade sucks on the crook of my neck, his tongue swirling in circles against my skin and making my nipples tingle as I imagine his tongue giving them the same treatment.

Lex slides his hand up my thigh, lapping at my folds with his tongue as his thumb finds my clit and teases it until I'm squirming against Kade's hold. His tongue plunges into my pussy, and I moan, reaching for something, *anything* to hang onto. Kade's hands find mine, and I lace my fingers through his.

Lex pulls his hand away from my clit and uses both hands to hold me open to him, his tongue bouncing between sucking my clit and plunging deep into my pussy until my head is spinning and I'm gasping for breath, writhing against him.

In minutes, I'm racing toward orgasm, my heart pounding in my chest and the muscles in my thighs tightening as I reach climax and cry out, squeezing Kade's hands until my knuckles are white and moaning loudly.

Lex leans back, grinning at me as he licks his lips and heat fills my cheeks. Kade frees one of his hands from mine and curls his finger around my chin, turning my face so my lips meet his, and he kisses me deeply. When he pulls back, I'm desperate to suck air into my lungs. As my body vibrates with electricity and pleasure, still riding the aftershocks of my orgasm.

When Lex stands and heads toward Atlas, my eyes widen, but Gabriel quickly replaces him in front of me, the bulge in his boxers distracting me from watching what Lex is going to try with Atlas.

I pull my other hand free from Kade's and reach for Gabriel—more specifically the waistband of his boxers to pull his cock free. Excitement fills my stomach and my core continues to throb as he lowers himself onto the couch, but instead of kissing me, his lips meet Kade's as he lines his cock up with my entrance and pushes into me with ease. I slide my hands up his bare chest, holding him and getting lost in the scene of him and Kade exploring each other's lips. His cock pushes in deeper, hitting a particularly sensitive spot, and I press my lips together, moaning once more. He pulls nearly all the way out before thrusting back into me. He finds a steady rhythm, rolling his hips and hitting a spot deep inside me over and over that has me panting in a matter of minutes. He pulls back from Kade's mouth only to seal his lips over mine, and I lose myself in the feel of his lips as he picks up the pace of his thrusts, and Kade reaches between us circling my clit with his fingers.

It doesn't take long for another orgasm to rack my body, leaving me a trembling puddle of pleasure. I don't think I could stand if I had to at this point. Gabriel slams into me a few more times before the muscles in his thighs tighten, and he grunts, shooting his release into me and kissing me hard.

I manage to catch the scene of Lex going down on Atlas past Gabriel's shoulder, and my pussy clenches around Gabriel's cock at the sight of Atlas's head bent back against the chair, his eyes shut, biting his lip with a look of pleasure etched into his usually sharp features. I don't know what it is about the sight of the most powerful vampire I've met in that position, but when Gabriel moves inside me again, I'm overcome with another orgasm, and I grab his face, bringing his mouth back to mine as my hips arch, trying to push him deeper inside me.

Atlas grunts across the room, gripping the arms of the chair until his knuckles turn white, and he shudders.

Lex swallows Atlas's release and rocks back on his knees, smirking at me over his shoulder.

"Perhaps we should move this into the bedroom?" Kade suggests as Gabriel slides out of me, dropping a soft, sweet kiss to my forehead.

Lex moves at vamp speed into the other room, and we all turn to look at him through the open sliding barn-style door into the bedroom.

Gabriel moves off me, helping me sit up, and Kade gets off the couch, following Lex's lead.

Atlas rolls his eyes, tucking his cock back into his boxers and standing, walking toward the kitchen instead of the bedroom. He comes back a minute later with a glass of blood in one hand and a bottle of water in the other. He hands me the water, and I take it, murmuring a quick word of thanks before unscrewing the cap and downing half the bottle. I set it on the coffee table and get up, somewhat surprised my legs are strong enough to hold me upright.

Gabriel slides his arm around my waist anyway, and I don't protest when his other arm curls around the backs of my knees and he sweeps me off my feet, carrying me into the bedroom, with Atlas trailing behind us.

Despite the massive bed, it's still a pretty tight fit for the five of us. I end up sandwiched in the middle, with Kade and Gabriel on one side and Atlas and Lex on the other.

Pressure builds in my chest as each of the guys turn their attention to me. My heart pounds in my chest, and this time, it has less to do with the orgasms that tore through me moments ago and more to do with the weight of the words on my tongue, daring to be spoken.

"Angel?" Gabriel murmurs, his eyes dancing over my face and lit with concern. "What is it?"

I swallow past the lump in my throat, then sigh softly. "I don't care about the blood oath," I finally say. "Despite it being the catalyst of what brought me to you, it won't be the reason I choose to stay." I take a moment to look each of my vampires in the eyes. "I'm not going anywhere, because as much as I *can* see my life and my future without the four of you, I… I don't *want* to. So whatever happens, whatever we're forced to face, it will be together. I'm here and I'm yours, as much as you are mine."

The following morning, the lot of us are sitting around the dining room table at breakfast. Gabriel made some egg frittata thing, and Calla insisted on walking down the street to a local bakery to pick up muffins, which Gabriel was more than happy to take her to do.

After her speech last night, the four of us are coming to terms with her decision to stay with us despite finding out that in terms of the blood oath, she had no obligation to and could be free of us at any time.

I'd never admit it out loud, but what she said made me want to wrap my arms around her and never let her go. She has certainly made our lives interesting these last two months and brought light into the darkness for all of us.

Gabriel's phone starts ringing as we're finishing up breakfast, and he sets his coffee down, answering the call on speaker. "Fallon, what is it?" he asks.

"Gabe, I don't want you to panic, because we're good, but we were involved in a little, uh… situation."

Gabriel frowns briefly. "What kind of a situation, Fal? What happened?"

"We were attacked by hunters," Jase says.

"Son of a bitch," I growl under my breath.

"What the fuck happened?" Kade asks.

"We were ambushed," Fallon says. "I don't know if the number of hunters in Chicago has increased all of a sudden, but it felt like every single one was in on this attack."

"How did you escape it?" Atlas chimes in.

"Yeah, that's the thing," Fallon says with a tone of unease. "Selene saved our lives."

"You're going to have to say that again," I tell her, "because I'm certain we did not just hear you correctly."

"Oh, no," she says, "you did. We would be dead if it wasn't for her. Needless to say, our cover is effectively blown, so I'm not sure what you want us to do now."

"Fucking hell," Kade curses, slamming his fist against the table.

"Did she say anything to you?" Gabriel asks, raking his fingers through his already messy copper hair. There's a haunted look in his eyes, and I'm sure his head is spinning as fast as mine is, trying to decide what the hell we're going to do.

There's a chance Selene didn't tie Fallon and Jase to Gabriel. I don't know that they ever met—I doubt it. But Selene was obsessed with Gabriel. She would know if anyone so much as breathed on him.

"It doesn't fucking matter," I chime in. "Just because she saved a couple of lives, it nowhere near makes up for everything she put Gabriel and Calla through. She's a dead woman."

Kade and Atlas both nod their heads in silent agreement, while Gabriel sits quietly. Calla stares at her lap, her jaw set tight. "I don't really know what to do with this information," she says in a low voice.

Gabriel sighs. "Are you sure you two are okay?" he checks.

"Yeah, man. We're good," Jase says.

"Do you know where Selene is now? Atlas asks.

"No. After she saved us, she took off pretty quickly. If you guys are going to come, now is the time. I doubt she'll stick around much longer, and we can't exactly go looking for her again without raising suspicions if we happen to find her."

"I'll call you back," Gabriel says. "Be safe." He ends the call, gripping his phone in his hand tight enough the glass cracks, and he drops it onto the table, cursing under his breath.

Calla reaches for him, wrapping her hand around his arm, and he lets out a slow breath. "I'm sorry," she says in a gentle voice.

He somehow manages to smile at her.

"You think she knew who they were?" Kade asks. "Could she have saved them with the thought of using it later to get back to you?"

Gabriel rakes his fingers through his hair, shaking his head. "I truly don't know. But why would she take off after saving them if that was the case?"

"Perhaps that's something you can ask her before I tear out her esophagus," I offer. "I think we better get back on the plane." There is no way in hell we're letting that psycho bitch get away again.

Atlas stands. "I'll call Marcel and arrange for the flight and have a car pick us up. Get ready and pack some clothes." He turns his attention to Calla. "I don't suppose there's any point in me asking you to stay behind?"

She regards him curiously. "You would ask?"

They stare at each other for a moment before Atlas sighs. "Never mind."

She nods, a hint of a smile on her lips.

In ten minutes, we each have a duffel bag packed and meet in the living room. We're about to head out when Atlas glances down at his phone, and his expression hardens.

"What is it?" Kade asks.

"New York is calling. We are being summoned—all of us."

"What for?" Gabriel asks.

Atlas shakes his head. "It doesn't say, but if I had to guess, it's probably about the hunter attack last night. Evidently it has garnered some media attention and there's some concern from the Capitol."

"What does that have to do with us?" Calla asks. "I mean, besides us having been there? What is there to say about it now?" Her voice is even, but she won't meet his gaze. Her pulse is also slightly elevated and sweat dots her brow. She's trying to project confidence, but I can see how nervous she is and I don't blame her one bit.

He blinks at her, his expression void of any emotion. "I don't know, but this isn't a suggestion."

"Right," she says, pressing her lips together, and doesn't add anything else.

"I'll call Fallon back and let her know we have to make a pit stop in New York before we head to Chicago," Gabriel says.

I lean against the back of the couch, sighing. I can't help but think this *pitstop* is going to be a lot more than that.

I've only been summoned to New York with Atlas one other time and that was shortly after he sired me. Lenora and Simon made it known they weren't happy Atlas had turned me and also made it very clear that Atlas's position in this world was more important than I would ever understand. It didn't matter Atlas had little desire to participate in the politics of their world—they refused to allow anything else for their son.

So here we are, heading back to the Big Apple to face what is sure to be a complete shit storm.

❄ 20 ❄

CALLA

I can only recall ever being this scared twice in my life. The night the vampires came for me and when I thought my mom was going to die.

There's a black town car waiting for us at the airstrip in New York when we land, with tinted windows and men in suits standing outside. One opens the door to the back seat, and we pile in, Gabriel and Atlas on either side of me, with Kade and Lex in the seats behind us. No one speaks—the car is deafeningly silent as we drive away from the airstrip. The car ride feels simultaneously too long and too short. I keep my hands on my thighs, pressing my fingers into my skin so my knees won't bounce. I don't know who the guys in the front are, but if they're affiliated with Atlas's parents—which I figure they must be—I can't show any sign of weakness, despite the way my heart pounds, causing my pulse to race.

I considered I would eventually be forced to meet the scary, all-powerful York vampires who produced one of the most difficult and intimidating people I've ever met in my life, but I certainly wasn't prepared for it to be today.

Atlas keeps his gaze trained forward, his jaw set in a tight line. His stone cold demeanor sure doesn't make me feel better about the situation.

I pull my bottom lip between my teeth, chewing it absently as I stare out the windshield. When I taste blood, I tense, my eyes widening. *Shit, shit, shit.* I didn't get a good look at the men in front of us so I'm not sure if they're vampires. My anxiety heightens tenfold, and I jump when Gabriel places his hand over mine on my thigh, my gaze whipping toward him.

He leans in, his lips brushing my ear. "They're human," he whispers. "Breathe, angel."

I close my eyes, trying to focus on the warmth of Gabriel's hand on mine, grounding me. Despite my aversion to glamour, part of me wishes I'd asked one of them to use it on me to chill the fuck out. Pulling in a deep breath, I turn my head slightly so my hair acts as a curtain to my face, then let it out slowly.

"That's it," Gabriel murmurs, gliding his thumb back and forth across the top of my hand. "You're okay."

"I'm freaking out," I admit in a hushed tone.

Gabriel sighs softly. "I know, but I need you to trust that we're not going to let anything happen to you. Can you do that for me?"

I hesitate, pressing my lips together. Not that I have much of a choice in the matter, but I appreciate Gabriel's words. And when my chest tightens and my breath hitches, I come to a realization that somehow makes me even more anxious. "I trust you," I say, swallowing hard. "All of you."

Lex and Kade both reach for me from the back seat, each of them touching one of my shoulders, and I turn my gaze toward Atlas to find him already looking at me. His expression softens ever so slightly, and he offers a subtle nod. There's an understanding between us that, at this moment, requires no physical touch.

And oh my god, I am so damn screwed because, despite my best efforts, I've fallen for him—for all of them. The knot in my stomach tells me there's no coming back from this. Whatever happens, these guys—these equally lethal and caring vampires—are my future.

Not much later, we pull off the main road and continue driving, thick forest lining both sides of the vehicle. There isn't another car or building in sight, and we eventually slow to a stop in front of giant wrought iron gates. The driver rolls down the window, speaking too soft for me to hear to a woman stationed there in an all-black uniform.

A moment later, there's a loud clicking sound, and the gate slides open. We drive through, and my breath catches when my gaze falls upon the house we're driving toward. *House* isn't the appropriate word for this place. It's more like a palace compound and looks like something out of a movie. It's ridiculously huge and impeccably landscaped, with a long reflection pool leading up to the front of the building where our car slows to a stop once more.

The two guys up front make no move to get out, and a third man in a suit walks out of the building, heading toward the car, and opens the door at Atlas's side. "Mr. York," he greets in a level, polite tone. "Good to see you, sir."

Atlas nods at the man but says nothing, getting out of the car. At the last moment, he finds my hand and squeezes it once without looking at me, and I think it's meant to reassure me, but the mess of nerves in my stomach don't know how to react.

I slide out of the car behind him as Gabriel gets out the other side, with Lex and Kade following after me.

"I'll have someone collect your bags," the man says, still only addressing Atlas. "Your parents are waiting for you inside."

Atlas nods again and starts toward the building. The four

of us follow him, Kade and Lex on either side of me, with Gabriel taking up the rear. They are essentially caging me in between them, which should make me feel safer, but right now, I'm suffocating. If this meeting is about the hunter attack, my presence doesn't make all that much sense, considering I'm not a vampire or a hunter. Which makes me think my being here is due to some creepy fascination the Yorks have with their son's human... whatever I am, and that really doesn't make me feel better about the whole situation.

We walk up wide marble stairs with massive pillars on either side, and I don't think I could feel more wildly out of place anywhere else.

The man who greeted us opens the tall, glass door, holding it as the five of us file inside what I am reluctant to call a foyer because of how ridiculously huge and fancy it is. The marble from outside carries in and the ceilings are at least two stories high. Directly in front of us is a staircase leading to the second floor and an intricate chandelier hanging from the ceiling. On one side of the lavish entrance is a sitting area with a white stone fireplace that sits unlit and a sleek black grand piano. The other side has several sets of doors, all closed, and stunningly detailed canvases hung between them—oil paintings, I think.

"Mr. and Mrs. York are in the formal dining room," the man announces.

Gabriel touches my back gently, guiding me forward, and I follow Atlas down a brightly lit corridor, my Docs echoing softly on the marble floor. I wipe my palms on my thighs and pull in several deep breaths, but it does nothing to help the anxiety in my chest, making my pulse pound beneath my skin.

We stop outside a set of solid black double doors, and the man opens them, stepping aside for us to walk in.

The space is just as fancy as the one we came from.

There's a long, dark wood table in the middle of the room with chairs set around it, and at the head of the table is a man nearly the spitting image of Atlas, though he appears maybe twenty years older than the vampire at my side. My heart slams against my ribcage and my feet stop moving. Terror grips my body, and I wish nothing more than for the floor to open up and swallow me whole.

The woman to his right is the most stunning person I have ever laid eyes on. Lenora York has long auburn hair, striking silver eyes, and sharp features like Atlas. She's dressed as if she's attending the Met Ball, and I can't help but glance down at my own clothes. I nearly laugh at how ridiculous I look in comparison. Her eyes travel over us, focusing on me for a split second before landing on Atlas. Her lips curve into a subtle smile, and she stands, smoothing the front of her red wine colored dress. She moves away from the table, gliding toward us with graceful ease. "Atlas, my son, welcome home." She stops in front of him, kissing each of his cheeks.

"Mother," he says in greeting. "I'm afraid we can't stay long. There's a matter we need to attend to in Chicago."

Her brows crease and what could be misconstrued as concern passes over her features. "Chicago?" she asks, sounding mildly disappointed.

"Yes. Gabriel's sire is there, and we would like to deal with her before she can leave the city."

"I was under the impression Selene was residing here in New York, which was the reason for your previous visit."

My heart skips a beat, and I pull in an unsteady breath. Something tells me she wouldn't take too kindly to knowing she was lied to.

"No one likes her, so she moves around a lot," Lex says in a dry tone, and my eyes widen slightly, but I stay silent, my jaw clenched so tightly it's causing my gums to throb in protest.

Lenora purses her lips, clearly unamused. "I see. No matter, we appreciate you coming to us on such short notice. Please allow us to handle the issue in Chicago. I would hate for it to take you away so quickly."

"That won't be necessary," Atlas says, his voice is smooth but firm. It's hard to believe he's speaking to his own mother. There's no love or fondness in his voice. It's strictly business. "I'm sure we can settle whatever is going on here and be on our way shortly."

She frowns, turning to Gabriel, who she reaches her hand toward. He immediately takes it, stepping forward, and brings it to his lips, brushing them over her knuckles. "Lovely to see you again," she says in a softer tone than I was expecting to hear from her.

Gabriel nods. "A pleasure, as always. I apologize that our business elsewhere must interfere with this visit."

She pulls her hand back smoothly and smiles at Gabriel. "Nonsense. I understand your sire has caused many issues for you and I will be happy to have her handled."

I watch Gabriel's face, though he gives no hint as to what he's thinking.

"I, of course, appreciate your generosity," he says, "however, I must insist we deal with this particular issue ourselves. Selene has caused a great deal of anguish, and though I cannot personally deliver the action against her that she deserves, I need to be there when it happens."

Just when I expect her to refuse him, Lenora nods. "I understand. We will have the plane ready to take you there after our visit. Please, come sit. We were just about to eat." She moves down the line toward Lex, leaning in to kiss his cheek, then does the same to Kade, pausing in front of him. "I understand you lost your sister during a recent hunter attack."

Kade's eyes widen, as if he wasn't expecting her to bring it up. "I... Yes," he finally says.

She nods. "And you killed the hunter responsible?"

A muscle feathers along his jaw as his gaze darkens. "I did."

"Good." With that, she returns to the table where her husband is standing at the head. No sympathetic words or comforting gestures. Just *good*. She doesn't even acknowledge my presence, which, not to sound self-absorbed, but I figured was kind of a big deal. I'm not about to complain about it— I'd be more than happy to go unnoticed this entire visit, though I have a feeling that's not going to happen.

We walk over to the table, and Atlas takes the spot to his father's left, shaking his hand before the rest of the guys do the same, which leaves me standing there feeling absolutely ridiculous. I'm not sure how I'm supposed to address these people. These vampires, they're royalty in their own world, but from the things I've heard about them, I'll dislike them as much as I'm terrified of them.

"And you must be Miss Montgomery," Simon says in a deep voice. His gaze slams into me, and my entire body fills with discomfort. I want to step away—run away, actually. But I force myself to stay where I am and nod.

"Calla," I say, thankful my voice doesn't crack.

He offers me his hand, and I hesitate before placing my palm against his, and he covers it with his other hand. "Charmed to meet you."

I force a smile and murmur, "Thank you," because what the fuck else am I supposed to say? It's not exactly nice to meet him too, and I'm not about to lie to someone who can kill me with a subtle flick of his wrist.

The corner of his mouth quirks slightly as I've seen

Atlas's do on occasion, and he releases my hand. I let it fall back to my side, fighting the urge to curl it into a fist. My eyes shift toward Lenora who is watching me with a look of distaste. *Perfect. She already doesn't like me.*

I inhale slowly through my nose and say, "That is a beautiful dress, Mrs. York." The moment the words leave my mouth, I want to kick myself. It sounded stupid to my own ears, so I can't imagine what the rest of the room is thinking. *Why am I complimenting this woman?*

Her eyes trail the length of what I'm wearing and a smile settles on her lips. "Thank you, Calla. Perhaps I can find you something more appropriate to wear after our meal."

I bite the inside of my cheek to keep myself from saying what I really want to say and nod. "That's very kind of you."

"It is my pleasure, dear," she says in a voice drenched in haughty, fake politeness.

"Shall we eat?" Simon suggests, and we all sit around the table.

I pick the spot next to Atlas, while Lex sits on my other side and Gabriel takes the seat next to Atlas's mother as Kade drops down next to him. A moment later, a group of waiters file out of a door across the room, each carrying a different tray or bottle around the table. Wine glasses are filled with champagne and a second glass is filled with what I immediately recognize as blood. The waiter approaches my chair to pour, and Atlas moves before I can, covering my glass. Without a word, the waiter moves on and fills Atlas's glass. He pulls his hand back, and I let out the breath I was holding.

Next, the waiters bring out plates filled with lamb, seasoned potatoes, and a variety of steamed vegetables. Despite my nerves, my stomach growls at the decadent smell of everything, and we eat in silence for a while before Atlas speaks up.

"I understand the situation in Washington last night was not ideal."

Lenora stops him with a quick wave of her wrist. "We are dealing with that, son. It is nothing to worry about."

Atlas takes a drink of champagne, shifting his gaze between his parents. "I see." His voice is hard. "Then why are we here?"

Simon takes a drink from his glass of blood, setting it on the table and shifting his gaze from Atlas to me. I freeze with a forkful of potato halfway to my mouth. I set it down on the plate quickly and press my lips together. "You are here," he says, "because your mother and I thought it was important to discuss Miss Montgomery's place in your lives."

Gabriel clears his throat. "With all due respect, sir, I don't understand why Calla's place in our lives is relevant to anyone but us."

Lenora sighs, as if she's disappointed in him for speaking. "Gabriel, consider how it reflects on us to our people—those who look to us to set an example—when they catch wind of the four of you keeping a human pet."

My blood runs cold as my gaze snaps toward her, and I tighten my hands into fists under the table, my entire body tensing. I bite my tongue hard, stopping before I can taste blood, figuring this is not the best place for that to happen, considering I'm sitting around a table full of vampires.

"Sorry," Lex cuts in, "you're concerned about optics?"

She doesn't even spare him a glance when she says, "Essentially." Finally, she turns her attention to me, and I fight to hold her gaze, because what I really want to do is lunge across the table and slap her across the face. *I am no one's fucking pet.* "I understand the agreement that was made which outlined the plan for your future, Calla, has been nullified based on new information being brought to light."

"So what?" Kade cuts in. "Yes, the blood oath is void with

regards to Calla. She is free to do as she wishes and she wishes to stay with us. What does that matter?"

She lifts her chin, turning her face toward Kade. "It matters greatly, and you should know this by now. You have been well-acquainted with Atlas for many decades. At this point, you should understand the importance of his role in our society. This arrangement you have created with Miss Montgomery is not something that can continue as it stands." When her eyes shift back to me, I open my mouth, but she continues speaking before I have a chance to say anything. "You thought your future was tied to these creatures based on an agreement that was made prior to your birth. It is quite unfortunate you had to live any part of your life believing you had no control over your own future. I have sympathy for you in that regard, Calla. But, my dear, the oath is void. You are free to leave. That is the choice you should make."

I swallow hard, blinking against the sudden burn in my eyes. Anger heats the blood in my veins, and I straighten in my seat. "I have made my choice already."

"Hmm," she says, glancing toward her husband. "You see, that is a problem for us. The way you are now will not stand."

I lick the dryness from my lips, shaking my head. "I don't understand."

Lenora takes a sip of her champagne, sparing Atlas a brief glance before returning her attention to me. "It is quite simple. We are giving you two options. You can choose to be glamoured and forget about the vampires you have met along with everything that has happened since they took you."

"The fuck—" Kade snaps.

My eyes narrow, and I shake my head, cutting him off. "Yeah, no. That is *not* an option. Now that I actually have a choice in how my future will play out, I'm sure as hell not going to let anyone try to push me toward something I don't want."

"I understand," she says in a level tone. "Perhaps you will feel more motivated to choose the other option."

"The one where we get the fuck up right now and leave?" Lex says, his expression grim and his fangs fully extended.

"Sounds good to me," Kade adds, dropping his fork onto his plate so carelessly I'm shocked the porcelain doesn't shatter.

"Enough," Simon snaps, silencing the room.

My heart pounds so hard in my chest I can feel it in my throat. I grip the arms of the chair, and everything in me is screaming to run, to get as far away from these vampires as possible.

"There is no need for theatrics," Lenora says with a sigh.

"We are not going to force Calla to do something she doesn't want to," Gabriel says in a firm tone. His jaw is set tight as he looks at her.

She tilts her head ever so slightly, as if to question his stance. "Unfortunately, that is not your call."

I swallow the bile in my throat. "What are you saying?" I force out. "What is my other *option*?"

My stomach drops when her gaze flits to me, as if part of me knows what she's going to say before the words leave her bloodstained lips.

"Mother, no," Atlas cuts in with a sharp, venom-filled voice, making me jump.

Lenora tuts her tongue, barely sparing him a glance before she focuses on me once more. "Calla, you will either forget everything… or you will become a vampire."

END OF BOOK FOUR

Preorder book five at mybook.to/unraveledbydesire!

If you enjoyed *Fated in Ruby*, please leave a review on Amazon and Goodreads. Reviews are so important for authors to find new readers!

Sign up for the newsletter at www.authorjacarter.com/ newsletter-sign-up for book news!

Join J.A. Carter on Patreon at www.patreon.com/ authorjacarter for exclusive access to signed paperbacks, bonus content, early cover reveals and book releases, plus so much more!

Follow J.A. Carter on Instagram and TikTok (@authorjacarter) to stay up to date with all of the things!

Join J.A. Carter's Reader Lounge on Facebook for first looks and exclusives!

ACKNOWLEDGMENTS

To my incredible beta readers: Carolyn, Jenni, Diane, Haileigh, Kylee, Tyler, Charlotte, Cheryl, Jordyn, Kate, Lauren, Maddy, Sydney, and Sara.

To my amazingly supportive patrons: Haileigh, Ashley, Devin, Lauren, Meredith, Maddy, Juliana, Marilyn, Courtney, Jess, and Bianca.

And to you, my lovely readers. Your continued support means the world to me!

xx,
   J.A. Carter

Lightning Source UK Ltd.
Milton Keynes UK
UKHW040821200223
417306UK00006B/1125